DREAM

Borgo Press Books by S. Fowler Wright

Arresting Delia: An Inspector Cleveland Classic Crime Novel
The Attic Murder: An Inspector Combridge & Mr. Jellipot Classic Crime Novel
The Bell Street Murders: An Inspector Combridge & Mr. Jellipot Classic Crime Novel
Beyond the Rim: A Lost Race Fantasy
Black Widow: A Classic Crime Novel
The Capone Caper: Mr. Jellipot vs. the King of Crime: A Classic Crime Novel
Crime & Co.: An Inspector Cleveland Classic Crime Novel
Dawn: A Novel of Global Warming
Dead by Saturday: An Inspector Cleveland Classic Crime Novel
Dream; or, The Simian Maid: A Fantasy of Prehistory (Marguerite Cranleigh #1)
Elfwin: An Historical Novel
The End of the Mildew Gang: An Inspector Cauldron Classic Crime Novel (Mildew Gang #3)
Four Callers in Razor Street: An Inspector Combridge & Mr. Jellipot Classic Crime Novel
The Hanging of Constance Hillier: An Inspector Cleveland Classic Crime Novel
The Hidden Tribe: A Lost Race Fantasy
The Jordans Murder: An Inspector Combridge & Mr. Jellipot Classic Crime Novel
The King Against Anne Bickerton: A Classic Crime Novel
The Mildew Gang: An Inspector Cauldron Classic Crime Novel (Mildew Gang #1)
Murder in Bethnal Square: An Inspector Combridge & Mr. Jellipot Classic Crime Novel
The Police and the Public: Some Thoughts on the British System of Justice
Post-Mortem Evidence: An Inspector Combridge & Mr. Jellipot Classic Crime Novel
The Return of the Mildew Gang: An Inspector Cauldron Classic Crime Novel (Mildew Gang #2)
The Rissole Mystery: An Inspector Combridge & Mr. Jellipot Classic Crime Novel
The Screaming Lake: A Lost Race Fantasy
The Secret of the Screen: An Inspector Combridge & Mr. Jellipot Classic Crime Novel
Spiders' War: A Novel of the Far Future (Marguerite Cranleigh #3)
Three Witnesses: A Classic Crime Novel
Too Much for Mr. Jellipot: An Inspector Combridge & Mr. Jellipot Classic Crime Novel
The Vengeance of Gwa: A Fantasy of Prehistory (Marguerite Cranleigh #2)
Was Murder Done? A Classic Crime Novel
Who Murdered Reynard? A Classic Crime Novel
The Wills of Jane Kanwhistle: An Inspector Combridge & Mr. Jellipot Classic Crime Novel
With Cause Enough?: An Inspector Combridge & Mr. Jellipot Classic Crime Novel

DREAM

or

The Simian Maid

A FANTASY OF PREHISTORY

by

S. FOWLER WRIGHT

THE BORGO PRESS

An Imprint of Wildside Press LLC

MMIX

CONTENTS

CHAPTER I.

SHE looked at the magician with eyes that were bright and rather hard, and disputed the evidence of a dimple that came easily.

She was twenty-eight, and looked younger.

"It must be a dry cave, and large—and vacant. I hate snakes. I mayn't stay there; but, at least, I'll begin with a cave. I'm not going to find myself drenched with rain before I've had time to turn round."

The magician looked worried, and felt more so.

"My dear Miss Leinster," he said, "I'll do my best. But a dry cave—you know they're not common, except in fiction. And they're popular with so many creatures when they do exist. A dry cave, and vacant. I'll do my best. But—what would you say to a tree? A really good tree, safe and high?"

"But you said they were dreams?"

"So they are, and so are we, for that matter. They're as real as we are. The human mind cannot invent anything. I couldn't have given you a dream of Atlantis unless it had once been real, and you were there as really as anyone ever was."

"I don't understand," she answered, "and I don't suppose you do either. But I'm going to dream a dry cave for a start this time, or it's the last deal we have."

The magician raised a white and well-fed hand in a gesture of protest. "Miss Leinster!" he said, "have I ever failed in a promise?"

"No," she said. "I had the goods, and I've paid the price—and it only makes me resolved to go farther. I know our world from Tibet to the Amazon. Thanks to you I've seen Atlantis, and I've had a few months in Babylon. But I want something primitive this time. I don't care how primitive. And I want a safe place to start from."

She leant forward slightly, and her tone changed. "You might tell me this: could I get killed in a dream?"

He answered frankly: "I don't know. I don't really know much about it. I've found out some things that are new and seemed strange

7

at first, but they're obvious enough when once you get used to them. In a way, you ought to know better than I."

"Well," she said, "perhaps I ought, but I don't. When I was in Babylon, it seemed real. It doesn't seem like a dream now, when I think of it. I can still see Urdu's eyes when—" She stopped, and her own eyes became introspective, and her mouth closed firmly. There was no dimple now. Then she shook herself free of the thing she saw, and continued more lightly: "I hurt my foot while I was there, rather badly. It was my fault. I didn't understand the rules of the traffic. There was no scar when I came back—I don't know that there had been—but it used to hurt in the same place when I thought of it, and sometimes when I didn't. But, then, if they're only dreams—"

"I didn't say they were only dreams," he answered. "I should never say 'only' of any dream. We don't know what a dream is. But we do know this. When we dream, we see places that never were, and we meet people that never lived. We don't suppose that they know that we make them. But suppose a god were to dream. Wouldn't he dream better than we can? Mightn't his dream be vivid enough to give his consciousness to the creatures of his imagination? And isn't that what we are? I shouldn't say 'only a dream' if I were you; and I certainly shouldn't try getting killed in it."

She looked at him with amused and friendly eyes, and her lips curved into laughter. "I suppose that's why you like to be paid first. But you're always straight, though you're rather dear. I must trust you for the cave."

"Well," he said, "I won't let you down. I'll tell you if I can't find it just to your liking. But you must give me a clear week from today. I may have to go back a long time. But you shall have it primitive enough. It won't be safe—but you know that. Can't we compromise on a really good tree, with a cave to follow?"

"Well," she said doubtfully, "I don't want to be unreasonable. I suppose a dry cave wasn't often to let. If it's a good safe tree—"

The magician sighed his relief.

"You can see where you are from a tree," he said. "It gives you a better start."

"Yes," she said, but without enthusiasm, "perhaps it does. But suppose there's someone or something at the foot...someone who might do something un pleasant, without waiting long enough to talk it over when we get there together?"

"I have wondered," he said, giving no direct answer, "how you have got over the language difficulty?"

"I was meaning to ask you about that," she replied, "because I had two different experiences. I could not understand anything in Babylon. I never really learned their language the whole time. I was like a wild creature that has lost itself among city streets. The safest time I had was when I was awaiting sale in the slave-pens. But in Atlantis it was quite different. I could talk their tongue from the first. I knew all their ways. I felt and was accepted as one who had been born among them. They knew me by name, and yet I was myself, with my own memories. It was only when I refused to marry the King's nephew that they began to think that something was a bit queer. Ah-Tem, the psychologist, wasn't puzzled even then. He said it was a case of dual personality."

"He may have been right," the magician answered; "but such things are not easy to understand."

CHAPTER II.

IT was two days later—when the magician was busy in his private laboratory—that he heard a sudden noise of confused shouting in his outer apartment. He was not easily flurried, and he continued his occupation calmly.

At exact intervals of seven seconds he was dropping a golden coin into a sliding funnel, which carried it into a square, bronze-coloured cylinder glowing with heat, From a spout in the farther side of this a thin stream of molten gold trickled into an open bowl of a dull green metallic lustre, surrounded by scroll-work of intricate and snake-like pattern. The bowl must have applied an intense heat to the liquid metal it received, the source of which was not apparent, for from it rose a heavy vapour which was continually received by an overhanging cone, so that the quantity which the bowl held remained constant.

He had dropped in only two more of the golden discs, so that the interval was less than a quarter of a minute, before the door was flung violently backward, and a young man, very tall and largely made, burst into the room.

"Who are you?" asked the magician, in a voice that sounded cool and preoccupied.

"I want to know what the devil you've done with her."

The magician was not a man of exceptional physical courage, and he suffered from a flabby heart, the result of a long period of excessive eating, from which all his wisdom was insufficient to save him. He was aware that he was in some danger of physical assault, which he would be ill-fitted to resist, yet he had confidence in his own adroitness to avoid the danger, and he answered quietly: "Will you tell me who you are, and of whom you speak?"

"You know who I am well enough. What have you done with Miss Leinster?"

The magician ceased his occupation, and crossed the room to the seat which he usually occupied when receiving callers.

10

He motioned his visitor to a stool at the other side of the table.

"If you can show me that you have a right to inquire," he said reasonably, "I will give you any information which I possess."

"Then you do know, you—you lousy trickster! This is the third time, and if you think I'll leave this room till I know—"

"Do you observe that the atmosphere is not quite as pleasant as it was?"

"There's a foul stench about, if you mean that."

"Yes. It will get worse till I resume the work which you interrupted so impetuously. If I am not back at it within about fifteen minutes, I doubt whether either of us will leave the room alive."

"I shall leave this room when I damned well please, but I'll get the truth first, if I wring—"

"The door closes with a spring lock. You could not find the secret to open it in a week."

"Then get on with your work, and we can talk at the same time."

"I prefer not to do two things at once."

"Then tell me what I've asked, and I'll clear out."

"I don't know that you have any right to ask it."

"Miss Leinster is engaged to marry me in a month's time."

The magician looked surprised. "I should need proof."

His visitor drew a small folded note from his pocket, and tossed it across the table. "You call read that, if you like."

The magician opened it with deliberation. He read:

Dear Prince,

If I'm above ground in a month's time, it's a deal.

Yours,

MA

He looked up speculatively. "Are you a prince?"

"Am I a fool? That's a nickname, of course."

"Why do you suppose that I should be interested in your mother's letters?"

"In my—it's not my mother, of course. It's Marguerite."

The magician looked at the letter and his impatient visitor, and at the letter again.

"I thought," he said, half aloud, "that she was a sensible girl." His tone implied that a doubt had arisen. Then he remembered that she was no longer at hand. "Perhaps," he continued, "she is." He looked his visitor full in the eyes for the first time. "Mr Cranleigh," he said, "I will accept this note as authentic, and am willing to admit the interpretation which you would place upon it. It gives you some right to ask, and I will answer as well as I can. She has gone some distance to a place of which I cannot give you the address. It is a locality which is actually under water at the present time. And, all being well, she should be back in about a fortnight from yesterday."

The young man was conscious that there were heavy fumes in the room, and that he was breathing with an increasing discomfort, but he held to his purpose tenaciously.

"I want something better than that. That's how it's been twice before. She's disappeared for a fortnight, and come back looking fagged out, and no explanation of where she's been."

"Has she told you nothing?"

"She tried to put me off with silly talk about Atlantis, and Nineveh or Bagdad or somewhere, till I got sick of it, and gave up asking."

"Then she told you the truth. She has gone farther on this occasion" He saw angry disbelief in the eyes that met him, and he went on: "Mr Cranleigh, why do you suppose I accepted that note as meaning something that it doesn't say?"

"Because you knew better than to call me a liar."

"Not at all. If I thought you wanted Miss Leinster, and wouldn't tell a lie to find her, I wouldn't lift a finger to help you. I believed you because, if you had been offering something that had been made to deceive me, you would have contrived a more explicit forgery. Now, you are an engineer, Mr Cranleigh. You know that you must deduce accurately, or that the price of error will be inexorably exacted. If I were aiming to deceive you, should I not have invented a more likely lie?"

"Have it your own way. But you'll be good enough to have her back in the next five minutes, or to show me how I can go to the same place."

"You are asking a difficult thing. At Miss Leinster's own request I have given her a dream by which she will have a year's experience in a very primitive land."

"A year? You said fourteen days."

"Pardon me. I said she should be with us in fourteen days. Dreams may pass very rapidly."

"But where is she asleep?"

"I cannot tell you that. The physical body disappears in these experiments. I do not understand why. Yet that they are of the nature of dreams there can be no doubt at all."

"If you'd come to the point, instead of talking all this patter. Do you like this stench? If it's money you want—"

A cheque-book came to sight. A fountain-pen poised for action.

Whether it were the sight of the ready pen, or that the fumes were becoming too noisome for his own endurance, may not be easy to decide, but the magician's foot moved under the table, and the door-lock clicked, and the door swung open. There was a movement of icy air. Stephen Cranleigh had a feeling that it swept round like a sentient thing, or like a housemaid's broom. He drew in delicious breaths.

"Come with me," said the magician. He led the way to an inner room. He showed a couch, on which lay a woman's clothes, not folded, but still retaining her shape in a flaccid way, as though her body had been withdrawn without altering the form in which they had covered it.

"In about thirteen days," he said, "I shall expect to find her sleeping there, and that she will wake within a few hours of that time. She will have had her dream."

The engineer looked at the magician in a very sceptical bewilderment. He could not positively recognize the clothes. He was unobservant of such details. Possibly this might explain why he had wooed Miss Leinster for three years without persuading her to the point of marriage. But he recognized the frock to be of a shade of red which he knew she wore.

"Will you swear she's safe?" he asked doubtfully. And then, as the magician hesitated in his reply, "Can you send me the same way?"

The magician was slow to answer. "I don't see why you shouldn't have the same dream," he said at length.

"Does that mean that I should actually get to her, or is it a fake?"

He weighed his answer with care. "To dream in common, to dream the same dream at the same time, and to believe it true could there be a more effectual reality?"

"I suppose you can't help talking shop," was the impatient answer, as they returned to the laboratory. "How much will it cost?" He did not know what to believe, but he must take the risk. If it were all a silly bluff—well, he would know in a few minutes. It was true that no harm had been done to Rita the times before, and whatever had happened she had come for it again.

"It will be two hundred pounds," the magician was saying, "and twenty more for spoiling the experiment that I had in hand."

"Does that cover two?" said a girl's voice from the shadows beyond the door.

Stephen Cranleigh started at the sound. "Elsie!" he exclaimed. "How did you—?"

"The young lady has been here all the time," the magician interrupted. "She followed you in."

As he spoke she advanced to the table, and laid her left hand on the cheque-book that still lay open upon it.

"Will that amount cover two?" she repeated.

The magician observed her hand to be brown and thin and nervous, and bare of rings. It was such a hand as he should have expected from the slim, upright body and small dark head.

"Oh, yes, Stephen, I shall! I shall go if you do," she went on, silencing his protests before they were spoken. Her voice was coaxing, with a note of nervousness, but yet definite, as of one who had learnt how to get her own way in earlier battles. He would have been less a magician than he was had he doubted how that debate would end. He was admiring the dark, pleading eyes, and the fine chiselling of wilful lips, as he said hastily, "It will be four hundred and twenty pounds—but I suppose it ends here. I'm not going to do this for a crowd."

Stephen Cranleigh wrote the cheque.

CHAPTER III.

RITA sat in an outer fork of a giant tree in the forest. Its branches spread widely over the interval of a forest aisle, where the yellow rhinos had made their ancient path to the water. They would come along it in the evening, their young cubs sporting clumsily behind—cubs as large as the full-grown animals of the time from which she had come. But she did not think of that. She did not think of the size of the animals that would pass beneath her as extraordinary. Animals are large like that. They just are.

She did not think much about anything now. There is much to smell in the forest; so much to see; so much to feel; so much to hear; so much to taste. There is little time for thought, which is always dangerous.

It was a crooked bough that reminded her of something that she had seen before. Her mind struggled with a reluctant memory, as it might do to recall a dream.

Suddenly she knew. It was like a branch that had obscured the light of her bedroom window and that she had had cut down a few weeks ago. It was a branch that she had often watched as she had lain awake in the early summer mornings, in no haste to rise. A most familiar thing. Yet she had recalled it with a mental effort that was almost torture. Was she forgetting entirely? Her mind was shocked to an instant clarity. It had not been so at Atlantis, nor at Babylon. In those adventures she had been aware always that she was a temporary stranger, who would awaken to her own place and time. But it was different here. Was it that she was so much farther away? Too far for even recollection to bridge the æons that lay between? If her memory went, would she lose herself indeed? Would she fall from dream to reality and return no more? She was frightened at that. She would not let herself forget. She would repeat each day. The shadow was moving from the bough she watched. It was at the very edge. The forest was so still that it did not flicker on the edge of a swaying branch. It moved steadily, as though it were a shadow on the ground.

There was no wind which a tree could feel, but she could feel it through her hair. It had been coming from directly behind her, as a wind should, so as not to ruffle the glossy smoothness of the fur; but it had shifted somewhat to her right, and she had been slow to adjust her own position. What strange thing could have made her so negligent?

If the wind were not at her back, what security could she have? She was frightened that she could have been so forgetful. Some dream. But even in sleep—she must hold dreams in check, lest she die. Suppose that a tree-leopard—not that it would dare. But suppose it had.

Or suppose that one of the hated Ogpur—

She fancied hairy paws that grasped her arms from behind. Her head twisted round with so abrupt a motion that a tufted grub-catcher fled from the tree, mocking her voice as it gained the shelter of a great sycamore on the farther side of the forest aisle. She would be careful to keep her ever-consciousness of vision and sound and scent. She would not dream again.

The hated Ogpurs—they were creatures that ran upon the ground, hiding among the undergrowth, scraping under tree-roots, making holes like gigantic rabbit-burrows, feeding foully upon the flesh of the smaller creatures that they caught and tore with bloody nails.

They were not of her kind, though they might claim to be so. Nor were they of the kind of the cave-dwellers in the sea-cliffs, the lift of which she could see in the blue distance from the high perch she had chosen.

The Ogpurs were mongrels. They could not climb with the agility of her kind, and had she remained among her people, she would have regarded the idea of any danger from them with a light derision. Had one of them ventured to climb among her fellows he would have been the instant centre of a chattering, excited mob, flinging great nuts from every side upon his blinking eyes, even perilously snatching at hand or foot to dislodge him, that he might fall to death upon the distant ground. What use would there be in strength of arm or jaw against foes that he could never reach?

No, the Ogpurs knew their place. If they came out in the open spaces of the forest they did it at the risk of a hard-flung nut and a cracked skull. Only at the drinking-pools might they emerge in safety at the proper period of the day.

And their fate would be worse than that should they venture out to the open downs, toward the sea-cliffs where the cave-men dwelt.

Sling or catapult or throwing spear would send its message to meet them.

The men of the caves and trees might hate or despise each other, but the Ogpurs, who were the result of the crossing of the two breeds, were the contempt of both.

She knew that, should she consort with one of them, even though she were an unwilling captive, she would never be allowed to climb again among her own kind.

But she had little fear of that. Even here, alone, in the woods that were too near the cave-men's dwelling to be frequented by such as she, she had confidence in her own agility.

But what did she here alone when the spring had come, and she was of an age to have been seeking a mate of her own kind?

There was one.... She did not think with names, but by vision. We need not trouble about him. He will not concern us further. He was a rather fine specimen, darker furred than most. He had a broken toe on his left foot.

Had she felt the grasp of his hands upon her, firm and strong, she might have bitten, but she was not sure that she would have bitten hard. It is pleasant to be loved in the springtime. Very pleasant when you are young, and it is an experience which you have watched, but have been treated as too young to share.

But she did not anticipate such an experience. It was not etiquette for him to use force to obtain her. Not unless she should tease him to do it.

She knew that she could have had him had she willed; and, instead, she was sitting here, looking over to where the cliff-tops showed dim blue against a bluer sky.

But she was not sure what she wanted. It was not the way of the forest-folk to mate casually. Unions were for life, though they might commence with no more ceremony than a chase through swaying boughs, a cry and scuffle among the hiding leaves.

It was different in the caves. The cave-men might have more wives than one, might drive them out in anger, or even buy or exchange at a price. The cave-men were of a lower, hateful kind. They worked. They made implements. They hung grotesquely the skins of other creatures from their shoulders. They ate flesh and shellfish, dabbling in dirt and blood. They had made their bodies insufficient, so that they must carry things about with them when they moved. Evil, indeed, would it be for one of her cleaner, untoiling kind to be the wife of such as they. To live in a cave which could not be kept habitable (if it could ever be so!) without ceaseless labour. To move encumbered with skins. To eat food which must be scorched beside the fires that ever burned on the rock-platforms.

Rita cracked a nut between sharp teeth, and flung the shell to the distant ground, Fruit and nuts for her. Clean food that never failed. To eat and sleep, that was her life, and to sport in the sunshine. That, and to sit in the high boughs, vaguely aware of beauty, satisfied with sound and sight and the joy of living.

Yet she had come here, none having seen her go or being curious to follow.

She had come here to watch for a sight of one of these cave-men whom she could not wish to wed, and who, she feared—and it may have been the strongest urge that had brought her here in this futile folly—had lacked the sense to admire her.

She did not doubt that she was a very beautiful woman. She was taller than some of the men. She had a secret belief that there were no longer arms in the forest. More than one of the boys with whom she had played in earlier years had evaded her challenge of measurement.

Her body was covered with a seal-soft fur that lay so close and light that it looked like a naked skin. Only the palms of hands and feet were bare, and—she moved slightly to scratch one of the callosities on which she sat; they were of a brighter colour than the fur, and she was inwardly vain of their beauty. She remembered how she had half turned that he might have a better view, and he had not seemed to observe them. The bat-eyed fool! No wonder she had leapt into the trees without a backward glance that might have called him to follow. Anyway, he couldn't have followed her through the boughs. What had such as he to do with the forest? He said he liked me in red and I got it to please him. He never noticed it at all. And he couldn't understand why I wouldn't go out with him the next night. He looked like a dog that's been beaten and he can't tell why. Only sulkier.

The thought moved dimly on the threshold of her mind; moved dimly, and went out.

Why did he come into the forest, where even the cave-men, with their killing-tools in their hands, were not safe—not one or two alone, anyway—from the snarling, lurking Ogpurs?

There was no answer to that.

She sat till the sun was at its noonday height, and then she began to move through the trees.

When she stopped she was about a mile nearer the sea-cliffs.

She sat there during the heat of the afternoon, cracking nuts, which were very abundant even at this time of the year—for the cave-men did not climb the trees, only gathering those that fell in their season, and the forest life avoided their vicinity. The time when mankind would become an earth-wide curse, from which all other life would crouch and flee, might be a million years ahead, but its shadow was beginning to move already upon the face of the world.

As the afternoon waned, and the silence of the empty forest continued, she moved again, and when she stopped she was nearer still.

CHAPTER IV.

THE Law-maker sat in the inmost cave, which he had not left but once in a dozen years, for he was of a great age, and his life must be guarded vigilantly.

Twelve years ago, when he had been challenged to fight for the place he held, he had survived the duel, but his success had been one part craft and two luck, and he had seen that in the faces round which had warned him that others would soon be bidding for the same stake.

He had lain awake that night, hearing the noise of the feast that celebrated his triumph, which he had been too exhausted to share, and he had seen that he must contrive some safety for himself, if his life were to continue. Was it for nothing that he had been known from boyhood as the Coiling Snake?

In the morning he had moved his precious things into this inmost cave, which was lighted only by the pine-wood torches that were fastened round its walls.

The approach to it was a low passage through which a man must wriggle for a score of yards, for it was too low for hands and knees, nor would a fat man get through it at all.

He had had four old wives who had been his from his youth, and on whose fidelity he could rely; for who else would keep them as he did? He had two young ones that he had taken to supplement them in recent years, as a man must, if he lived long. He was sure enough of them also.

One or other of these wives was always squatting vigilantly where the passage opened to the cave, a stabbing-spear in her hand. That was the greeting for any, man or woman, who came unasked; and there had been more than one who had learnt that it was no idle threat.

There had been incidents and changes in the twelve years.

Two of the older wives had died.

One of the younger ones had attempted to leave him. She had been but a few yards along that wriggling passage, making slow way, for lack of exercise and plenteous food had made her girth too great, when she had felt a sharp pain in the calf of her left leg. Other pains had followed.

What was the use of haste when the Law-maker was shooting arrows into the mouth of the passage as rapidly as he could fit them to the bow—arrows that could not fail to be stayed by some portion of her desperately wriggling corpulence?

She had emerged with half a dozen showing their feathered shafts, as though they had been shot up from the ground beneath her.

She had lived two days, and then been knocked on the head by a kindly cousin, who, before he did it, promised her that she should have revenge. Then they had dropped her body into the sea from the cliff-top, though food was short, and she would have made excellent eating, for the Law-maker had forbidden them the flesh of the tribe, and there was none who dare break his laws, even though they might design to destroy him.

The cousin had proposed a plan which had been readily adopted. It seemed simple and quite sure. The Law-maker was little more now than a dreaded name. He was seen by few. It was easy to be bold in the sunlight.

There was water in the cave; but suppose they withheld food? Those who stayed inside the cave would die. If the Law-maker came outside, he could be challenged by whoever would, and his end would follow.

So it was tried.

But the Coiling Snake had foreseen this danger. He had stored much food. For months he made no protest, and there was no suffering in the cave.

He had hoped that the plot would cease, but it did not do so. The blockade continued.

At last he must try the only chance that remained. He sent an ultimatum that, unless food were supplied within seven days, his wife's cousin would die as she had done. It seemed a foolish threat, and the man laughed, but they doubled the watch at the entrance to the cave, so that anyone should surely be captured who wriggled out. But except the Law-maker and the three wives who remained, there was none in the cave. It seemed a very foolish threat.

Yet in the night the Law-maker arose. He knew a secret way from the cave, which he had kept from knowledge of all, even of his most trusted wives. Now two slept, and one watched at the hole.

None saw what he did. He climbed to a high ledge. He squeezed into a narrow cleft. He had a bow in his hand.

Half an hour later he was in the cave where his enemy slept, with his head on the tanned pelt of a sea-beast. There is little noise that can be made when such a pelt is wrapped over the head, and drawn with a tight thong. He was told that he would die if he cried, and he lay still. Then his hands and feet were tied, and he was so muffled that he could not cry if he would. Then the Law-maker shot six arrows from the foot of the bed, choosing their places with care. After a sufficient time he untied the hands and feet. He loosed the pelt from the head. He left all as it had been, except for the arrows in the dead man.

The next day food came.

* * * * * * *

The Law-maker was a wise man, seeking the good of his tribe. In the silence of the cave he thought much.

He did not intend to be starved by the cousin of a false wife, or to be killed by any, but while he lived, he would contrive the welfare of the tribe, even beyond his death.

He sent for his son, Stele, who was now grown, and for Elsya, his daughter, both being children of his favoured wife, who still lived. They were two he could trust.

He said to them, "You are son and daughter of mine, yet you are no more than others, for the law has been that he shall rule who is of the strongest arm, and he may be challenged by whoever will. Who is there that will seize the rule when I die?"

And Stele said, "There is Borl."

The Law maker said, "I would have you to rule."

Stele said, "Then I must kill Borl."

The Law-maker said, "You must try to kill Borl. You may fail, and my plan may fail also. Yet it is worth a trial. For I will that if you kill Borl, or any other who may be stronger than he, you shall then be secure. I will make a caste. And to that end I will make a law.

"You will go out and say that, though I may live for summers to be, I grow old. I will that you be my heir. Yet I would not break the old law. Let any who will make claim that he have the better right, and you will fight it out, as the old law is. If there be more than one, let them first fight among themselves, and you shall fight him that survives. By this means you will fight once only, and against one who may be wounded by then, and will have spent strength. I cannot do more for you than that.

"But that you shall be secure when you have fought this one fight, I shall make a new law that none shall be king hereafter if he be wed to any woman of his own tribe, lest he favour those of her kin, and for other reasons which I will set out in chosen words.

"You shall go to the tribe that is far to the south, beyond the river-mouth and the great bay, and ask their king for a woman comely and sound, who is of his near kin; and if he have a son who is fit to rule then we will give him your sister as a fair price, if that king shall agree that I have made a good law, and his son shall establish himself in the same way."

Stele answered to this, "I will do all that you say. But I do not think that many will be willing that the old custom die."

"Yet you will find it otherwise," said his father. "I am wiser than you. Have you a heart to be king?"

"I have a good heart to be king," said Stele, "for I have a plan to make a dam of felled trees, from which we should take much fish, and it needs the labour of all, but they will not hear."

His father was pleased at this. "You will make a good king. When are you of an age to wed?"

"By the law you made," he answered, "I am of that age next year, as is Elsya also."

"That is so," said their mother. For Elsya was two years older than he, and the law was that the women must remain unwed for two years longer than the men. It may have been a good law, or a bad one, but such it was.

So Stele went out and told these words to the tribe. There was none who could be discontent, for all had the chance to make claim if they would, and if they lost they would die, and if they gained, was it not well that they should be made secure by a new law?

There were two who challenged beside Borl, but he killed them both, making it a light thing.

When Stele would have fought him, he said he must have a week's rest, for he was no longer fresh, and he thought that Stele would make a hard fight. There were murmurs at this, for it was beyond the law, but Stele said it should be so, thinking it a fair claim.

When the Coiling Snake heard, he was ill-pleased; yet he pondered, and said, "If it be well at all, it is very well. He may be a great king."

There was no fight when the week was done, for Borl was hurt at the fishing, catching his thigh on a hook of bone, so that it bled much. Seeing the blood that he lost, he said, "Let Stele have it, for I am but dead if I fight, being so hurt."

So the plan proved good to that point; but when Stele went to the south country, he came back having fled through the night, and he brought no bride.

CHAPTER V.

THE Law-maker drowsed on a bed of skins, for he was weary of years. Also, he did not know whether it were night or day, for no light came to the cave. For twelve years he had seen no light of the sun, and of the moon once only.

The mother of Stele came to his side. She said, "He has come back, but he has brought no bride. He says that—" She went on for some time, making the best she could of the tale on her son's part, not knowing if she were heard.

When the time came that she paused, needing breath, Coiling Snake answered her.

"Has he no words? Let him tell the tale for himself."

So Stele came to his father's side.

"Have you fared well?" said the King, putting the woman's talk aside, as though it had not been.

"I have not fared as ill as I might, having brought back my life," his son answered. "I could not wed such as they. I would rather wed an Ogpur woman, with the wet dirt of her burrow caking about her loins."

"What is wrong?" asked his father. "They are people of your own blood."

"I know not how that may be, nor what is wrong, but they are of a dead white colour, like an evil frost, they are blotched with sores, and their women are weak at the knees."

Coiling Snake pondered at that. "It is the food," he said, as one who talks to himself, "for the ground that is behind their cliffs is bare and high, and the jerboas, which we catch on our downs, do not live south of the river. Neither have they the nuts which we gather once a year under the forest trees, going together so that the Ogpurs flee. Nor have they the goats' milk which we feed to our babes when their mothers are with child again. But they have shellfish there beyond count, so that they are not awake to their loss. This means war, if they have the courage to strike."

Stele did not deny that, but he had seen their men, and he thought it a small thing.

His father went on: "You have done well. Yet will not alter a good law. You cannot wed with the Ogpur trash. You must go farther away."

"There are the women of the trees," Stele said doubtfully. "They, at least, are clean."

"It is a child's thought. They are clean enough; but they are not of our kind. For one thing, they have no brains. They do not work, nor dress, nor make tools. They have few words. For another thing, you would not get one to come. She would not eat of our food, nor would she sleep in a cave. We might catch one, and keep her with gyve and lash, but you want something better than that. Besides, what would there be at your death? It is of such matings that the Ogpurs come."

Stele answered, "It is all true. Yet I have seen one that seemed of a fine kind, though she was overlong in the arms, as they are too apt to be. Also, I had a thought that, had I chased her, she would not have run too hard. Yet I may have been wrong in that, for while I looked she made off."

His father said, "It is foolish talk. She would scorn your ways, as you would hers. You must look farther away."

Stele agreed to this. He made several short expeditions into the forest, seeking signs of any people such as themselves, or for open country that might be crossed with speed.

He found little to give him hope.

At last his father said, "I grow weak, and the time is short. There are men in the world on the far coasts, and beyond the trees. You must go out, not returning till you have found a bride, either by barter, or force, or wile. You shall take Elsya, that you may have that with which to pay if you will, and that there may be a watch when you sleep. If you leave her, you will have bought a wife, and she can watch in her turn."

Stele said that it was a good plan, though he should sleep ill if he were watched by one who came not of her own will. But his father answered to that, "You know little of women, being young. There are few that will not hold to your part when you have dealt with them as a man should, be they loath or fain. Yet if you find such a one, and would sleep in doubt, you will break her neck in good time."

"It is a good thought," said Stele, and went in a very cheerful mood to gather his killing-tools, and a light fish-net which Elsya could carry.

Yet he spoke to his father again before he set forth.

"How will it be if you die while I am far off? There will be no rule in the tribe."

The Law-maker answered, "None will know if I die; for I will give orders that none come into the cave. Yet you will do well to speak to Borl that he order all that has been in your hands if you be long away. For he will do it, whether you ask or no. But if he do it at your charge, he will not seek it for himself, being of that kind."

It was early morning when Stele set out, making such way as he might under the forest trees, and holding the Ogpurs in scorn.

Elsya walked at his side.

Rita saw them, looking down through the high leaves, though they saw nothing of her. It was an evil sight that he walked with a woman thus, and anger rose in her heart. Yet she knew that they were no more than cave-dwellers, taking their women and changing them as they would. Also, she was not sure that he walked with a wife.

Curiosity would have caused her to follow had she had no livelier motive.

Watching all that day, she guessed their relationship accurately. They were familiar; but they were not lovers. They were of a like carriage, with a resemblance in face and gesture, and in the darkness of the hair on their skulls (for they were otherwise very bald, as far as their skins showed), having similarity in many ways, though he was large, even for a man, and she, being a woman, was of a lower stature.

Rita could not guess why they should wander thus. They gathered nothing but for a passing meal. They hunted nothing. They seemed to have no purpose but to get lost in the woods.

They slept side by side, on a grassy patch great tree and a stream's bank, and Rita slept branches above.

There was a full moon, rather low in and the sky was pale to the dawn when came.

CHAPTER VI.

RITA slept ill in a tree's fork. She was not used to wandering thus by night. In her own tree she had made herself a platform of plaited boughs and a canopy from the rain. She knew that it might be taken by others if she left it long.

Yet she had a mind to see more.

She could not have followed all the day as she did but that Stele kept ever to the trees. There were open glades of high grass, which was of twice a man's height at its most. These were of a width to be measured in miles, but Stele knew that the rhinoceri fed on the open plains, and were not easy to see when they were lying down, being of the yellow of the tall grass when it is in seed, or when the sun has scorched and the wind dried it; and it is their habit to trample all living things that come out from the trees, though they will not eat them when they are dead.

So, heeding naught of the Ogpurs, he had kept to the trees.

Had he been alone he might have justified his contempt, for these creatures were not careless of their own skins, and they might have thought him a prey too dangerous to attempt, either for the flesh on his bones or for the things he carried; yet these last were a strong bait, for they could make use of any tool or weapon that fell into their hands, though they would not make them, nor would they encumber themselves either with clothes or with the carrying of anything, unless it were for a settled object.

But Elsya was a different matter. For a woman either of the caves or the high boughs to walk the forest paths was to invite capture, and the Ogpurs had learnt that once she was in their hands she was there for life. For the men of the trees and caves were alike in this, that they would have no woman among them who had once been in the power of the Ogpurs, lest she bear a babe of mixed blood. And the women knew that should they return from an unseen adventure and bear a babe showing the Ogpur teeth (as it surely would), it would be very quickly thrown to the ground from the high boughs, or to the waters below the cliff, which few mothers would care to see.

It was the weakness of the Ogpurs that they had no leaders, nor any spoken laws. They lived in their own burrows, and they foraged each for himself, or for his own young. They lived like rats, lurking under the thick undergrowths of the forest. They could stand upright if they would, but they crawled much. They could run on their hind-legs, with the body bent forward from the hips, and the arms swinging ahead, but they relapsed to the ground when the need for motion was over. It was against their habit to stand or lie in an open space.

But though they lived so, and each was for himself, they would go back if they found that to be done which was beyond a single strength, and call others to aid. There may have been some who had done this, but it is less than sure, for the two had walked far during the past day, and must have been seen by many who would take their trail, though at a slower pace than they had used, not loving the open paths.

However that may have been, it is a fact that, during the later hours of the night, there was a gathering of Ogpurs in the dark bushes that fringed the stream, both behind and ahead. It was at this time that Elsya watched, for Stele had given her the privilege of the first rest.

She had roused herself reluctantly, for she had been heavy with sleep after the exercise of the day, yet for several hours she had watched well, being alertly conscious of the dangers of the night in this unfamiliar place. She was of the temperament which can meet a seen foe well enough, but is nervous of the unknown. She had very good hearing, and, as the night passed, she became aware of stealthy movements in the darkness around her. She wished that they had fire, but they had thought that a supply would be too difficult to carry.

She would have given much to be back in her cave, even though she should have lost the prospect of being sold by her brother as bride to a king's son, as she hoped to be. Yet there was nothing definite enough to justify her in disturbing his rest.

As the hours passed, though the sounds did not cease, she became less fearful, thinking that, whatever might be round them, no attack was intended.

The time came when she was aware that the dawn was near. She was to wake Stele when the sun showed, which was not yet, but she saw the pallor of the disc of the setting moon, which told that the greater light was advancing upon it, though it might yet be under the horizon line.

With the relief of feeling that the night was over, she dozed where she sat, and waked to find that she could not scream for the Ogpur claws that were round her throat.

She was pulled backward to the ground, and it seemed for a moment that she might have been dragged away in a silence that would have left Stele unawakened, when they might have killed him in his sleep, or been content with the prize they had taken, in which case he would have waked and found Elsya gone, and looked round for a time, and then gone on his own way (for what could he have done then that would have been worth doing?), and there must have been great difference in the events that followed.

But Elsya, though she could not loose the stranglehold from her neck, yet fought as hard as she might, and so far rose to her feet that she was able to draw up a leg and give a backward kick, with a great strength, for she had no will to be taken; and though she was one who walked little, she swam much.

The kick went home to a good place, and the Ogpur screamed, so that it may be said that Elsya gave the warning which a watcher should, though it was not through her own mouth.

Stele waked quickly. There were no Ogpurs round him. Their first aim had been to remove Elsya in silence, and there may have been an unwillingness on the part of each to withdraw from the chance of the greater prize, about which they might soon have been fighting among themselves.

Stele had a good bone-headed spear and a stone axe, heavy and sharp. This axe had been his father's gift when he left. There was nothing like it in all the land.

The spear went through the Ogpur that had screamed, from side to side. He was having more than his share. He loosed the girl's throat at that, as he well might.

Stele let the spear go. He fell to work with his axe. Elsya was willing to do her part. She tried to pull out the spear.

Rita had been awake for some time. She had been roused first by the stench of the Ogpurs, which was unpleasant, and of which she would have been aware at a much greater distance.

She watched the stalking of Elsya with interest, seeing it clearly in the dim light. She had no thought to interfere.

There was a moment during which it seemed that Stele had an easy victory. He felled two with his axe, and their screams rose. The others drew back. Elsya had time to pull out the spear. She came to her brother's side. They had their backs to the tree.

The Ogpurs faced them in a circle which was beyond their reach. Gathering thus, they became conscious of their own strength,

for they were like rats in this, that they had a kind of corporate courage such as they did not possess separately, and which increased as
their numbers grew. They came on with a rush.

Stele struck quickly and hard. I dare say he was the tallest man
of his tribe, though he might not yet have come to his full strength.
He was twice as tall as any Ogpur, and three times as strong. He
struck hard with the axe in his right hand, while he flung them off
with his left. Their teeth caught in the skins he wore, which saved
his flesh. Bones snapped where the axe fell. For a moment it seemed
that he would scatter them, but they were too many for that. As he
smote one, another got its teeth in his sleeve, hindering his next
stroke. They came on with a second rush, and he went down beneath
them.

Elsya fared worse than he. She did the best she could with the
spear, getting it well into the groin of the first that came, but she
could not recover it in time to be of any further aid. It was too long
for close fighting, nor was she trained in its use.

She went down, and Rita watched that she was drawn into the
thicket, and the way she went.

Now a strange thing happened to Stele as he fell, for he looked
up through the branches, and he saw Rita where she sat like a white
ape by the tree-fork, and it seemed to him that he was not Stele, but
Stephen Cranleigh, and that what he saw there, in the half-light of
the dawn, was not one of the tree-folk, but Marguerite Leinster,
whom he had given proof that he loved well. The next moment she
was hidden from him, for his face was covered by the belly of one of
the leaping Ogpurs, and he must seize this creature round the body,
drawing it down with all the strength that he had, lest the others
should get their teeth to his face and throat. For a moment they had
impeded their own attack by the numbers that had rushed upon him
as he fell. He was conscious of a suffocating mass, beneath which he
kicked as hard as he might, and of teeth that worried at the leather
garments he wore. And then he was free of the weight, and he felt
the ribs crack that were within his arms, and he flung his assailant
from him, and came to his feet, for the fight was done.

The fantasy that had come to him a moment before had left his
mind, but he saw what had been, and from where the help had come.

For when he had looked up as he fell Rita had sat with a nut-
pod in her hand, which she had plucked when the Ogpurs had come
out, but from that time she had sat watching the fight, too interested
to interfere.

Now these nut-pods were black and smooth, and almost round,
and of the size of an orange. There were six kernels in each, not

unlike the sections which an orange holds. But these pods were not soft and light, like an orange. They were as hard as stones, and very nearly as heavy.

They were the greeting which the tree-folk always gave to the Ogpurs, should they venture out from their burrows, or from the undergrowth, in the daylight hours. Rita had known this game from the time when she had swung perilously by one arm from her mother's neck as they made their way through the branches.

She saw Stele's face as he fell, and though his thought did not reach her (or she did not know, if it did), she took a good aim, and threw.

The nut struck one of the leaping Ogpurs on the skull, and he went down. The next nut struck another on the back of the neck, and there was a dead weight across Stele's knees. The third brought one down that was already loping to cover. There was no need to throw more. They knew well that the nuts were death.

Stele looked up, conscious of some bewilderment. He looked round for his sister, and started to find her, as a man should. Not knowing which way they had taken her, he started in the wrong direction, and was stayed by a cry overhead. He did not know the tree-language. He had a belief that there was little to know, but the gesture which his eyes met was unmistakable. He turned, and was warned back again. From the great height at which she sat, Rita could see the commotion which still continued where Elsya was being dragged away. It was not far, for these things had happened in a little space.

She knew that the thicket was alive with his enemies. Should they pull him down in a dim place, as they well might, she would be less able to help. She ran out to a branch's length, throwing far and well. There was scanty cover at the spot at which they strove with their reluctant captive. They took the hint, and went. Elsya came back. She was somewhat scratched, she had a bite on the hand, and her bruises were many, but she was not badly hurt.

CHAPTER VII.

THE need for many words does not depend upon the number of human thoughts, but their divergences.

It was true that the tree-folk had few words. They had sounds for love and pleasure and fear; for anger and pain and warning. Most of them conveyed feelings rather than facts, and they were all in the present tense. The rest would be understood by those whose lives were alike. There was mother-talk of a kind; and there were wooing sounds which were understood by those who were most concerned; and there was the mating cry, which was exultant on a high note; and there was the talk of lovers in the years that followed, chattering or crooning, and with no thought that they had any shortness of words.

The cave-men had more words, having more need, being (as was obvious to Rita) of a lower kind. They worked, they made, they wore, they carried about. Probably these things were necessary to them. They were of a lower kind.

Yet she would have been glad of words when Stele signalled to her to come down from the tree, and she would not move.

She was tempted more than she knew. She would have been glad to explain. She really wanted to flirt.

She did not think that the invitation was of a hostile or treacherous kind, but it was not natural to her to leave the trees.

Also, she could not forget, now that they were so close, that he was of a lower kind than herself, living in huts and caves, eating flesh, fighting and killing each other for greed of the things they hoarded—useless, foolish things, for what is life worth if it be spent in the bearing of weights when we move, or in ceaseless guarding of such things as are too heavy to be carried with ease?

She remembered also that they were observed to change their wives, fighting at times concerning them, and having many or few, as their strength or craft prevailed over their companions.

She saw that if she came down she would be in the power of this man; and though she followed him as she did, she was more afraid of his friendship than of his hostility, now that the time of choice was upon her.

She had no mind for any temporary association, being as monogamous as a monkey, or, let us say, as a chimpanzee.

She was the more repelled as she watched the two at their morning meal. For, after some discussion with Elsya, which she could not understand, Stele cut some chops with his axe from one of the Ogpurs, which they ate raw, having no fire; Elsya doing her full part, for, though of a slim build, she was one of those who eat well, and the women of her race attached a mystic value to the eating of flesh above all other foods, as they have done at all times, even to our own day.

So Rita kept to the trees.

They went on that morning through the forest, meeting with no adventure that we need pause to watch, for we have still far to go, and our tale is ahead; and at midday they came to a valley, great and wide, sinking very gently to a river that flowed through it, and showing distant hills, wide rather than high, on its farther side.

Now they must leave the forest, if they were to go forward at all.

Elsya said, "What will she do now?"

For one who sought a bride in a far land, Stele felt more interest in this question than can be considered wise. He had recognized Rita as the one whom he had seen before, and of whom he had spoken to the Coiling Snake. He might conclude, with some reason, that he excited her curiosity, and possibly a warmer feeling. Yet she kept to her own place.

They looked up, and she was out of sight.

They were not likely to know what she would do, for she was in doubt herself.

She had climbed to a tree's height to see that the plain was safe. She looked for a herd of rhinoceri, but she saw none. She knew that they were too huge to be hidden, and she knew that, wherever they were, there they would stay through the day's heat. So that, if the plain must be crossed, there could be no better time.

From her height she watched them start. They looked back and saw her. Stele motioned to her to follow. There was no doubt of how he felt.

Then Elsya did so. She could not be expected to share his feeling, but she would do her brother's will. Also, she was a generous girl, and this strange, unclad tree-creature had saved her from a life among the Ogpurs, which she was glad to miss.

Yet Rita would not come, though, being a woman, she did not go back either. She sat in the tree, watching them move through the tall grass of the plain.

She still saw them when they were miles away, and still she did not know what she had a mind to do. She was conscious of a great misery and a great doubt.

Then she heard a movement beneath her. A man of the cave-people came out from the trees, his killing-tools in his hands. His eyes were on the trampled grass, and he hunted an easy trail.

Rita could not guess why he followed them. She knew nothing of the purpose which had brought Stele and his sister forth, and even that might have been little help to this problem. Neither, if he came with a hostile aim, could she be of any likely help, being but a weak thing at a distance from her familiar trees.

Yet, after a time, though in trembling fear, she came down, and followed through the trodden grass.

CHAPTER VIII.

RITA walked straightly and well, for she had been taught in childhood, as all her people were, to stand upright, running along a level bough with outstretched hands, till, in time, though the branches swayed, she could walk thus, having her hands where she would. It was a tradition of her race that they kept their uprightness of form, though their arms might lengthen, showing that they were not born of the trees, but had come from the ground, as those seeking a higher life.

She had rested long, and she could make a good pace, which was well, for the man she followed took no rest, but she kept close enough, tracking him by the sound of his feet in the grass, for she could hear far.

Her own walking was very quiet. She had no need for a better pace than that, not wishing to catch him up. So they came to the river.

Rita was thirty yards behind, or it may have been more, when she heard him stop, and she stood still, listening well. The grass amid which she stood was too high for her to see anything but the sky, which was blue and white with cloud, and a few yards ahead, where it was broken by those who had gone before.

Hearing that he moved, but did not go forward, she thought, "It is the river," which brought a fresh doubt to her mind, for she could not swim.

Then she made a new way through the grass for herself, moving to the left, which was northward, for their way had been to the east—the sun, which was now low, being behind her back.

The grass became shorter as she went on, till she could see ahead, and it was the river indeed. It lay very broad and quiet, having little current, but shining in the light of the level sun. The ground sloped very gently toward it, becoming stony, and meeting it as a level beach, having no bank at all. In time of flood it must have spread far.

Rita did not think of that, though she was well aware that the ground had been sloping gently downward for a half-mile past. She looked at the river's width, which was worse than had been her fear, and she wondered what its depth would be.

She sat down to think, choosing a spot where the grass was still of some height, for she did not wish to be seen by him who must be near at her right hand

Sitting thus, she became aware that her feet ached, for they were not used to the level ground, and she curved them inward till the toes and heels were but a short space apart, so that they might rest while they could.

She felt desolate and afraid, and was more than half minded to return. But she thought that the way back would be too far to traverse before the darkness fell, which gave her a sharper fear.

She looked over the water, and she saw that the land rose gently toward the distant hills.

The sun shone on a low shoulder of hill, bare and green, about five miles ahead, and her sight, being as it was, she saw those two that she followed, taking rest on the ground.

She was not the only one who had good sight, for the man she followed came along the edge of the stream, his eyes being on the same spot. She would have been plain in sight had he looked, and she saw that he carried a fishing-spear in his hand and bore a flint-headed club at his girdle.

She had no weapons but the strength of her hands and teeth, and she knew that if his eyes should be turned her way she must be his, either as mate or meat, as his will chose. Her heart beat like that of a handled bird; but, beyond that, she was very still, making no movement at all.

The man did not look her way, having other thoughts. He fastened the spear aslant across his back, so that it would be clear of his limbs. He waded into the stream.

Rita looked, and courage came back to her heart. There were stones between him and her, and she could throw well. He was swimming now, and she knew that she could hit the back of his head so that he would sink, though it would not be an easy mark as the distance grew, for he swam low. Yet she did not do this, feeling unsure of all. She did not know that he was at enmity with those she followed, and he would do no harm to her now. She let him live.

She saw him come out of the water on the farther side, and shake himself for a time, his skin being wet, but he did not stay long for this, going on again at as good a pace as before.

Rita got up to follow. She did not know why she did this. It may have been that she was resolute to give warning to those that were pursued. She thought on the man's face, which she did not like. That proved nothing, for she did not like the looks of any of the cave-dwellers—except one.

Her feet had become stiff while she rested, and ached worse than before when she flattened them on the level ground.

She came to the waterside, not expecting to be able to get through it, but of a mind to try. She remembered that she had seen trees in a fold of the hills beyond the bare bluff on which she had seen them camped. They might be reached before dark. So, not knowing the impulse through which she moved, she waded in.

It was shallow at first, and then, suddenly, it became deep. She stumbled, went under, and rose with difficulty, finding the water to her neck. She tried to wade back, but the depth between her and the shore was too great. She must have come in by a somewhat different way, the current, however feeble, doing its part.

She kept her footing with difficulty, feeling the ground round her, and only seeking the shallower place, without regard to whether it led her farther from the shore she left.

This should have taken her back, but it did not do so. It took her to midstream, and then she found that she was out of the water to her waist, and could wade with ease to the farther shore. She was glad when she came to land, and went on again at a quick pace, having forgotten the aching of her feet.

CHAPTER IX.

NATURE has placed in the hearts of all men, in their dealings with women, an optimism incalculable and incurable, such as it has placed in the hearts of some women also in their dealings with men—some, but not most. It was true a million years ago as it is true today.

Amul had three wives, of whom one was barren and two were shrews. He was a man who would have enjoyed beating his wives. That might have been well, for there are women who enjoy being beaten, and there are others who are easy to beat. But his wives were not of those kinds. Rather, they were united against him with a threefold strength that he feared, though they might quarrel among themselves. They chastised him with tongues. If he replied with the only argument that he knew (for he was slow of speech), they did mean things while he slept. Things that are best untold. Much.

Yet Amul's thoughts had been on a fourth wife, and he had counted that Elsya would be his when her age of marriage should come, in the next fall of the year. Thinking it probable that Borl would be chief of the tribe by that time, he had bought his friendship with the best fish-hook he had, before any other had spoken for Elsya at all, for he was a prudent, far-sighted man—one who would dry fish in the season when the nets were full, and a storer of many nuts, being foolish only with women, as some are.

Borl had agreed, for the fish-hook was a great gift, and the thing in itself was good.

He saw that Amul was a man of full age, needing a young wife; for it was the wisdom of the tribe that such matings were best, as it was that a man's first wives should be mature in years, for it was from such that the hardiest children came; and this instinct persists in the race to the present day.

It was otherwise with the tree-people, who would have said, had they cultivated the folly of words, that matings should be for life, and that both should be young at the first, or how should they endure as they ought, which is an opposing instinct that has also endured in the race to the present day.

If we suppose the Ogpurs to have been the ancestors of the men of our own kind (and there is much evidence of character, of habit, and of physique to support this theory), then it becomes easy to see how these contending instincts may bring misery to our own young.

But Amul's foresight had failed. Borl was rejected from any hope of chiefhood, and Elsya was removed from the marriage claims of the tribe.

No one minded this, except Amul, for the truth is that Elsya was not greatly esteemed. She had the name of an idle, capricious child, such as might make a wilful and wasteful wife. She had hunted shellfish since she could walk, and there was none that could dive so deep nor remain under water so long; but that was not for any use, but that she might find the small white stones that were sometimes inside the shells, so that she now wore a double string of pearls on her sun-browned neck. And this was the more foolish, as her body was not a thing to be looked at with any pleasure, either by women or men, being lean and narrow at the hams, making it the greater wonder that she could swim as she did.

So it might be thought that Amul, having blundered thrice, was saved, by circumstance when he would have blundered again; but he was not disposed to this view.

Borl laughed.

Amul thought over that laugh in the night, while his wives slept. It is the fair reward of those who are mated as he that they have little fear of anything outside their own doors. Amul thought of a plan. He could retrieve the fish-hook by stealth, but he could not use it afterward. Borl was too strong. He could not use it if he stayed here, but—it was a wild plan. It excited his mind so much that he was still awake when the dawn came. He looked at the wife who slept nearest, and he saw that she was haggard and stringy, being of an evil temper, such as ages a woman faster than the going of years. He looked at the next, and she also was of a meagre and skinny kind. He did not look at the third, knowing her too well; and we may gain by that which he had paid much to learn. When he considered the sleepers, the plan was a much better one than it had been before. He rose quietly to steal the hook.

CHAPTER X.

AMUL did not start till the morning after that on which Stele and his sister set out. That was doubly wise, because none would connect his disappearance with theirs, and that which he willed to do was best done far away. He planned it for the second night. He counted that he would travel faster than they. He carried nothing at all except his weapons, and the fish-hook of which we know, because it was part of his plan to kill Stele in the night, and then he could take all that he had. Till then let him bear the weight.

For Amul had had a great dream when he lay awake in the night. That was the way of the cave-men. The tree-people dreamed only while they slept. That was why the cave-people worked and quarrelled, carried and wore; why they were of a lower kind than the tree-people. They had been discontent with life as it was, and having made it worse they were more discontent still.

Amul's dream was that he should go forth and never return, that he should kill Stele and take his sister, as he had meant to have her before. Wandering in strange ways, he thought that it would not be hard to find a couple or more of women whom he could add to his household, or, if he came on a peaceful folk, he could buy them with the pearls that were on Elsya's neck. He had heard that inland folk would give much for such stones as those, and he knew that women are cheap to the world's end. For then as now, men took the risks of life, so that they died, and there were always less of them than of the women. And so women were cheap. That was the price they paid.

Such was Amul's dream in the night. He would found a tribe.

* * * * * * *

There are few times when a man can forecast how a thing will be, and say after that it was so; or, if there be such, they are things on which he lies still.

If he move to shape them to his own end, there will be one thing that will not be just as he thought—a thing that may be small in itself, but will change all.

Amul had thought of those he trailed as camping in an open space, and he had considered that a watcher cannot look all ways at once. He had not thought that they might find shelter under a shelving rock, so that one could sleep secure while the other sat with a shelf projecting overhead and looked out at the night.

Or, at least, should so have looked out; but Elsya was weary. She had the first watch, it being her turn, and when Amul crept up, very quietly, the moon being covered by a great cloud, Elsya sat with her chin on her knees, which her hands held, but her eyes were closed.

Had it been Stele who so slept our tale had been soon done, at the price of a reddened spear, but Elsya was one that he had no will to hurt. She sat there, her hairless body covered with the skins of beasts (for it was not the custom of her tribe to take them off in the coldness of the night), showing a head of black hair that was very thick and glossy and short (for she had found that long hair would catch the weeds when she dived, so that she kept it cut short with the labour of many hours, hammering it between two stones); and Amul, looking, was well content, for though she was somewhat thin, she was not skinny, as were the wives he had left, and the pearls gleamed on her neck.

Amul could have done with her very well for that night, and he cursed the chance that she was not the one that slept in the rear. Still, she would keep. He was a cautious man, not one to lose his life in foolish haste. He resolved to withdraw. He did not know that Rita was but two yards behind him, nor was there much cause for trouble in that, for she was in a deadly fear. Had she been in the trees she had feared little, being of a natural courage, but here she knew that she had neither weapons nor speed, being at the mercy of all. Her heart beat like a caught bird, as it had done a few hours before, yet she had been resolute to come to the place she feared.

Yet he did not find her there; for, as he resolved to withdraw, the moon shone suddenly where the cloud broke. It shone full on to Amul's face, and Elsya opened her eyes and saw.

At the first moment she showed neither surprise nor fear. It was the way of men (and women) of her time to wake quickly and wide. She gave no sign that she saw. Yet she was of the mood to kill, if she could. She guessed why he had come.

So far we have looked at him from the inside. We have seen his dreams. We must look at him with Elsya's eyes now.

She saw a man ugly and mean-featured; crafty enough, which is good in its way, but of a kind that would use its craft (if it dared) against those of his own house, rather than against the stranger that is without the gates. One (she might have thought) who would take her necklace to buy other wives.

She saw more than that. She saw Rita behind him. While she puzzled as to what that might mean, and how best she should wake Stele, he lifted his spear as though to cast it upon her.

Elsya was not disturbed. She did not think he would throw. Probably he meant no more than to frighten her into silence; but Rita saw the movement also, and did not interpret it with an equal sureness. She caught the shaft of the spear from behind, and Amul was a startled man.

His first thought was that it had caught in some impediment of earth or tree. He swung round very quickly, wrenching the spear as he did so. Seeing a human foe, and having a very clear perception of the trouble which would be upon him from the other side, he used all his strength. Rita's arms were not weak, and she held on also with the strength of fear. Naturally, the spear broke.

Amul had no time to turn the weapon. He thrust with the broken shaft, and felt it strike bone. As he did this his troubles ceased.

Elsya was not a woman of war. She liked to sit by herself. Even a fight with another girl was a thing to avoid, if she could. For this weakness she was a joke in the tribe. It was not thought that she feared overmuch, having courage in other ways, though of a nervous kind, which there were few around her who understood. There was a girl who wore a string of the precious pearls which had been given for peace. As to that, Elsya had always been content in mind, for she was a girl who bit on the face, and Elsya had no will to have her face spoiled, of which she thought more than others would have allowed for truth. After that the two became friends, through a strange chance, but it is a long tale, which we may leave to itself.

But if Elsya was a lover of peace, yet she was not slow at this time. She did not pause to waken Stele. While she watched Amul in a still silence she had thought just where the stone axe lay. This she seized as Amul turned to recover the spear. She sprang forward, and struck. Amul fell where he stood. It was the end of his dream.

Stele waked to a finished thing. He looked down on the body of Amul. "Am I never to sleep?" he asked in a natural wrath.

He saw the body stir. He looked at Amul's wound, by the light of the moon, which still shone. "It was a poor stroke. Elsya," he said, "Is that the best you can do? You should be whipped for that."

We have seen that he was a man of strength. He took Amul by the two feet. He whirled him three times round his head and he cast him far. He went back to his rest.

The moon clouded again. Elsya sat watching as before. She did not think that it had been a bad stroke. She thought she had done rather well. But brothers are like that.

Her thoughts turned to Rita, of whom she had seen no more since the axe fell. She did not know she was hurt. She considered that she must have followed them over the open land. It was a very strange thing. She must be seeking Stele. That was plain enough. Yet she kept to herself. Elsya had a practical mind. She saw that they had a very watchful ally. She had a sympathetic imagination also. When she had gazed into the night for another hour, she understood the position. Not very well, perhaps, yet it was clearer to her than to either Rita or Stele. When her jealousy was asleep, as it was now, she was of a generous kind. She decided that she could coax Rita to join them, not doubting her power. She knew that she could persuade better than most, though she might fight ill. A wife more or less would do Stele no harm. She was not greatly concerned about the new law, though it pleased her well to think that she should be sold as a prince's bride. Of course she might change her mind when she saw the prince; but, if so, she would find a way for her will. She had belief in her own powers.

She waked Stele and went to her own dreams, which were of a good kind.

CHAPTER XI.

IT got colder during the night, when the sky clouded and a wind came from the north.

Stele walked for warmth before the dawn came. Elsya waked chilled and stiff. They were used to a cave's roof and a fire outside, and it was colder today than yesterday.

They ate what was left of the Ogpur steaks, and they talked of fire, which they wished they had found means to bring.

Elsya said, "We must rub sticks, at the worst."

"You may rub sticks till you tire," Stele replied. "But will you get sparks?"

"Yes," she said. "I shall go on till I do."

"Or your arm might fail, or you might sleep."

Stele did not look hopeful. They knew it could be done, but they had not done it themselves. Fire could always be borrowed. It was a proverb that it was better to walk far than to try the sticks.

It could be done also with stones. But it was better fun to watch some one else than to try yourself.

Elsya was not urgent to prove her skill. She said, "We shall get colder if we sit here. Should we come to a bleak land, if there are men, there will be fire that we can ask or steal."

They got up to go.

Stepping out, they saw blood on the ground.

They looked, for they had not thought that Amul had been so hurt that he bled much. Elsya picked up half of a broken spear. Its point was bright, but the jagged end of the broken shaft showed blood and some clinging hairs. The hairs were very short and fine, and of a very light colour.

"It is the tree-woman," she said. They looked around. The ground was bare, except for some crawling shrubs of a prickly kind, which would not have hidden a goat; but it was uneven, so that they could not see far.

Stele said nothing, though his eyes searched.

Elsya spoke again. "She would seek the trees."

"I cannot see what she does here," said Stele.

Elsya laughed at that. "You know well enough," she said, and he was silent again. They saw trees in a fold of the hills, about a mile away. Stele set off in that direction, looking round as he walked.

They saw blood on a stone, which told them that they came the right way.

Farther on they came to a place where there was much blood.

"She stumbled here," Elsya said, "where the ground falls, making the wound bleed again. Here she lay for some time."

Stele said nothing to that. Why talk when they both had eyes? That was a woman's way. Yet he looked for a longer time, and added the one thing which Elsya had not said, though she saw it as soon as he: "She has not long left." They went on.

Making a straight path for the trees, they came to a place where there was a hollow in the ground and a stream ran over stones. There was a steep bank on the farther side.

"She would not climb that," Elsya said. "She was too much hurt." Yet they could not see her nor any trace, since they had left the place where she had been.

Elsya spoke again: "She is not far off." They began to search up the stream, and so found her almost at once, for she had not gone far, but had turned from the straight way.

They thought at first she was dead, for she lay with her head in the stream; but they saw, as they came close, that the water was very shallow, and though the little waves broke over her mouth, it was only covered at times, so that she could breathe well enough.

The wound was in her left side. There was a long tear, and a rib showed white to the sun. All beneath on that side was dark with blood, which had run down to her foot.

Elsya was first to kneel at her side. She would not put her fingers into the wound, knowing that dirt kills, but she pulled the sides apart, so that she could see in. Rita moaned at that, though she did not wake

"She will not die," Elsya said. Stele agreed. They were wise of wounds, having seen enough.

"But she will if we leave her here." Stele did not dispute that, though it was less sure. He was looking at her with more interest than he meant to show. He had a thought that she was more beautiful than the women of the caves. Certainly she was more graceful of form, though he thought that her arms were too long. He was not sure that it was not better to be clad in a golden down than to be a clothes-rack of skins. He knew that the people of the trees had no brains, and it may seem that she had shown this plainly enough in the way in which she had followed him there; but he did not look at it quite in that way. He was not sure that his father's plan was as good as he had thought it before. He was already aware that the law that he would not be old enough to wed till the next year was of an exceptional folly. If he were old enough to fight Borl for the tribe's rule…. What he said was, "She would be a damned weight." (But he spoke a more emphatic vernacular.)

Elsya was amused again. She had known what he would do, but she made a diplomatic reply, being of those women who will humour children whether old or young.

"To most men it would be too much; but it will be little for you, you are so strong."

Stele only grunted at this. He turned her over, gently enough. He handed his spear to Elsya, with other things. He put both hands to her waist, grasping under the wound. She went over his right shoulder, the head hanging behind.

Elsya said, "It is bleeding again."

"It will soon stop," he answered, not over-content in tone.

She was heavier than he had thought. But he liked the feel of the bare, warm, down-clad body that his right arm was raised to hold. He was less sure than ever of the wisdom of Coiling Snake.

CHAPTER XII.

RITA had not known at first that she was much hurt, the stunned nerves being slow to wake from a wound of the kind she had received. But, as she drew back into the darkness and watched the body of Amul twirling round Stele's head for the throw, she felt the blood drip on her knee, at which she put hand to side, and felt bone and a cruel pain which did not cease though the hand withdrew.

She was of the same courage as was Marguerite Leinster of a million years ahead, for personality does not change, either from youth to age or from life to life, or, if it does, it is a very gradual thing. Yet with the knowledge of that wound, there came a panic fear that she should fall into the hands of those whom she had twice interposed to save. She felt that the ground moved as she walked, and she roused all the power of her will that she should not fail to reach the trees, which she knew were not very far ahead. She thought them nearer than they were.

The moon went from sight and the night darkened. Yet she kept straight enough, till she fell at a sudden break of the ground, and must rest for a time, waiting the strength to rise.

It was not only that she lost blood: she was weary from the toil of the last day, and she lacked food.

When she rose again, it was to stumble at every stone, and to walk in a crooked way, not knowing where she went, till she heard the sound of the water which was her greatest need. She had a hard effort of will to bring her to that place, and when she lay and drank, it was with a feeling that she had done that at which she aimed. With that feeling the strength of her effort ceased. Her heart slackened its pace. Her mind wandered to distant dreams, till she waked to know that her head hung between her downward arms, and that her face was against the skin of a dead seal on a man's back.

It is not a method of travel to be recommended in any circumstances. When the course is the uphill climb of a stony pass, and there is a raw wound to jolt, it is one to avoid with care. But Rita made no sound. She gave no sign that she was aware of the position in which she hung. Yet her mind was awake again, and alert to such sight as she could gain from half-opened eyes, and aware of every sound, and of the strength of the arm that was across her loins.

So they came to the head of the pass, meeting a cold wind, and a very desolate sight of barren hills and of a reed-fringed lake that was in that high place, very deep and clear, over which there was a wailing of birds.

CHAPTER XIII.

STELE said, "We can rest here and drink." These were their first two needs. He laid his burden down where there was moss among the stones. She lay without movement, and he looked at her with attentive eyes. "She could move well enough if she would," he said at last. "She hears all." There were some things that he knew.

Not understanding his words, or only in part, she was not disturbed. He looked at her pleased, and yet ill-content. Having carried anything so far, is it not yours?

He thought of food. "Are we never to eat again?"

"I have a piece of meat left," Elsya answered.

In the morning he had divided very equally what they had, though he could have eaten all. Now he had his reward. Elsya gave him most of that which she had saved. It was fair enough. He had walked a burdened way. And it was the custom of the tribe that the women went short first, if there were little for all. That was good sense, for the strength of the men must be kept up that they may hunt for more. There were some who held that exception should be made for those women who had a young child. There have been faddists at all times.

Having little to eat, Elsya looked to their companion—whether captive or guest was less than clear to the minds of any of the three. She washed the wound, using gentle hands. As she did this, Rita opened her eyes. They looked at one another for some time without attempt of words. Elsya brought water in cupped hands. She offered what she had left of the meat, from which Rita turned.

At the end of that time they were friends.

Rita, who could have done it very well before, sat up. She had regained some of her strength, but she had been panic-stilled, like a caught thing.

All she lacked was food, of which she had had less than her companions, and for which she had a more difficult need. She saw them casting their net, to try the chance of the lake. It meant nothing to her.

She thought it was a very dreadful place. The lake was black under a lead-grey sky. The reeds moaned. The birds cried, as though they wailed over a grave. She wondered that any should come to such a place, having known of a better life. It might be well enough for these others, for they were no better than cave-men after all. Nothing could alter that. How could she get back to her trees?

CHAPTER XIV.

BUT Rita did not go back to the trees, though for the next four days she had this purpose fixed in her mind. There were reasons why she delayed, though she had no doubt what the end would be.

In the first place, her wound was such that, though she could walk well enough (and did, for she would have no more of Stele's shoulder, even had it been offered with a good will, which did not happen, for he remembered her weight), yet it was less easy to climb. She found this at the first wooded place to which they came, which was no more than a copse in a vale that was steep and small, where she found nuts that she could eat, though not of a good sort.

In the second, Elsya was kind. She had no great cause to wish to keep Rita with them, but she was of those who will never seek at a slow pace or want in a pale way. What she would, she must. Having the wish once born in her mind that Rita should go their way, she would have given all that the world held (except her pearls) rather than that it should thwart her will. There are still those of this kind. They walk a hard way, finding joy at times, but no peace.

So it came at last that when Stele would have held to the high lands, that he might oversee the dwellings of men for which they sought, she was quick to say that Rita could find no food on the barren hills, though they two might fare well enough; and Stele saw this and went by a lower way. Yet he would not go down into the thick trees more than he must, for he would see first where he went, which is best done from the hills.

So they held to the lower slopes, and to little straggles of climbing wood, and for the first two days Rita saw none of her own kind.

Then they came to a gloom of great trees through which they must pass, as they had seen from the higher ground, for it stretched north and south beyond sight, though it was not very wide; and here Rita must climb, straining her wound, seeking food, of which she was in great need. And in the high boughs she came on a man of the trees who dwelt alone, having a roofed nest, and some platforms beyond, very great, so that she was amazed. She saw that she had come to a strange thing, as those who wander may do. But the man of the trees, having been alone many days (a long tale, which could be told, but tales are many, and we must go on with that which is ours), saw her to be a wife whom he would have if he could.

Rita saw a man who was strong and ugly and dark, with hair that was coarse and shaggy about his back. He was not at all to her mind. She did not like his teeth.

Beside that, she knew that though it is good to mate when you are young, it should be with one that you know well, after long playing in the trees. She had not been told this, for her people used little speech, but she had seen it from the time when she hung on her mother's back. Those who speak much may think speech to be of more use than it is. Rita knew the way of her tribe.

The man meant well enough in his own way, but Rita fled. She forgot her wound in her haste, and it broke and bled. Then she made poor speed, and he thought she was of a mind to be caught, which was not true. Yet, she being as she was, he would have had her, but that she made for the ground, calling on her new friends in her fear.

The man did not heed Stele. He may not have seen him. He followed Rita to the ground, being close behind. Stele came up and the man died. There is no need to dwell on that. It was hard on the man.

But this was a new thing—that Rita had fled from one of her own kind, and called on Stele for his aid. It gave him a new sense that she was owned by him.

But as to the tree-man being of her own kind, Rita would not have agreed. She looked down on him as he lay on his back, and she was glad he was dead, though she thought he had good arms. She thought that had he got his hands onto Stele, he would have gone back with a wife. It was much better as it was.

There was another way in which Elsya helped to keep the three together in the first days, though this she may not have known.

Stele had his eyes on Rita more than seemed to be a needful thing, and his thoughts more. Though she was not of his tribe, nor of his ways, yet he thought she would make a good wife. He thought that she was of a mind to have him, which showed her sense, and he thought he could have her when he would, in which he was partly wrong. Ever he became more doubtful of the wisdom of Coiling Snake and of the laws of his tribe. Every mile that he travelled away from these, the more easy it was to see that they might be less good than he had been taught to think.

Yet it was the law of his race that he was not yet of the age when he should take a wife, and he was pledged to his father's plan that he should seek one in a far land. What he would have done if he had been alone it is hard to say, but what he did must be in his sister's sight, which made such laws harder to break, though this he may not have known.

The fourth night was very cold. Rita was hungry and tired. She was strangely hot, and she had a pain in her lungs.

In the morning they had gone aside from the straight way, down into a great wood, so that she might get the food that she sought, but it had been full of a tree-folk that had given her little peace. They had had a war of their own, in which many of their males had been killed. She was chased by unmarried girls, who thought that she had come to the wrong place. In spite of all she got some nuts, and she showed that she could throw straighter than most, breaking a bone in the cheek of the one that had vexed her worst. Yet she had not fed well.

In the evening they came through a high pass. They looked down to a fertile land, and saw the dwellings of men of a new kind. But they stood on a height, meeting a cold wind and a cold rain.

Stele and Elsya cared little for any wind. They were clothed warmly in their dead skins, and they had been born in the caves of a bleak shore. They would swim the cold seas in the winter days. But Rita felt the cold of the wind, and the pain came as she breathed. She took no long hurt, for she was very strong, having breathed clean air from her birth, and the next day she felt well enough, being warm in the sun; but this night, when they found shelter under a low rock, and Elsya took the first watch, she was glad to lie close to Stele for his warmth, which she had not done before. He was clothed in the skins of seals which had been so dressed that they were as soft as when they had had their own lives, and Rita lay close, and was of a quiet mind.

But Stele was not of a quiet mind. He thought of the laws of his tribe, and they had never seemed quite so vain as they did then. "What is a wife more or less? If you carry a woman for six hours when she is hurt, so that your shoulder aches all the next day, is she not yours? Is she not yours if you kill a tree-man at her own call—a tree-man who had very strong arms, so that it was a dangerous thing to do? Is she not yours if she comes of her own will to lie close in your cave?

After a while Rita waked, and was aware that Stele's arm was round her. It was where she would not have it to be. She lifted his hand to her mouth. Her teeth closed on his wrist. He lay still, waiting to see what she would do. He knew the strength of her teeth, though they were not large. If she bit, he would be a man with one hand, and he would miss the blood that he would lose.

They thus lay for some time, and then she let the hand go, and they slept in peace.

After that they were better friends than before.

CHAPTER XV.

STELE looked at Rita and he was puzzled in mind. He could not see what she would have. She had come down from the trees. She had followed him all these days. Yet she would bite his wrist in the night.

He thought of her sex as being of a perverse folly and a curse to men. He was not the first to think thus, even in that day, nor would he have been the last in this. Yet it is not a very wise thought. It lacks depth. He did not see that Rita was in the same perplexity as himself.

She had that which she would be glad to sell, but she would be sure of the price. In the words of our own day, she would not have lust without love, and of the love she was not yet sure.

For there was a law in her tribe that all creatures have not learnt, though some better than men, as have the wild swans that will mate for a life's space, nesting in the Arctic peace.

It is a law that men will unlearn at times, boasting of better ways, but it must be learnt again, for it is one that will last till the world's end. It was a law that was better known by those of the trees at that time than by the men of the caves, who had the will to seek and to do; for there was more of wisdom in those who dwelt in the trees. They took the laws of God with accepting minds, as they took the sun and the rain; but the men of the caves had no doubt that they could take charge in His place. If we say that they may both have been doing His will in their own ways, it has the sound of a lively tale.

But Stele looked at Rita as they climbed down that morning through the pathless rocks, and he was a puzzled man, though he knew that they were of a better friendship than they had been before, which did nothing to clear his mind. Yet the will to have her for his wife was now a thing that he faced, even to the ruin of his father's plans, and as he looked at her the desire grew. Nor did he think of her now as of a wife "more or less," who is of little weight in the scale; he thought of her as more, and to be won at any cost that a man can pay.

It was in this mood that he looked down on the huts of men— huts such as he had not seen in his life before, being built of trees, solid and strong—and knew that he must be near the gates of a great king, such as he might approach for the giving and taking of brides, after the plan that Coiling Snake had devised.

They looked far down on a valley which closed up to a point at the north, where the mountains met. There were mountains on either side, steep and high, and the valley sloped down to southward between these walls, till it ended in a lake, which closed it from cliff to cliff. Stele saw that it was a very strong place. It would be a great thing if he could make alliance with such a lord, and if Elsya were sold as wife to its heir. He said this to her, and she agreed well enough, though she loved the shore, and as they had left it farther away she had been thinking that she should never love an inland life.

Still, there was a lake here. She could swim in that. She supposed there would be shellfish to find. There might be pearls of a new kind. She was uncertain in mind. She would wait till she had seen the prince, and then think.

What she said was, "How do you know what they are?"

Stele considered that. He saw that he did not know. He thought that only men would make such huts—so he said.

Elsya said, "I did not know that there are men who make such houses as that. Nor did you. It doesn't prove they are men. Men are not the only things that make homes. There are ants on land and many creatures in the sea who could do better than that. Not to talk of the birds.... I can see them moving about. They are not like men. They are too large, and they walk on all their legs. I don't think we should go down to them—not till we know more. I think I will stay here."

She sat down on a stone. Rita, who had been somewhat ahead, finding the way easier than did her companions, came back and sat at her side.

Stele was of a will to go on, being ever of impatient moods and eager to see a new way of life; yet he did not say she was wrong. There was another side to his mind, which disposed him ever to plan with care, seeing the end of his work before he should lift a tool.

He stood still with a frown. He said that women are a hindrance and a curse to men, though they will fight well among themselves. What could he do, having two on his hands to guard?

Elsya said, "Yet I killed Amul."

"It was a wretched blow. I would not talk of that, if I were you."

"It is your talk, not mine. It was a good blow enough. It was enough for him. I don't believe you ever killed a man of our own kind in your life, nor a woman either."

He was annoyed at that, because it was true. "How could I kill Borl when he wouldn't fight? Anyway, I shouldn't want to kill women. Men never do."

"No," said Elsya, who felt that the talk was going just as it should. "Men don't kill women, but women don't mind killing men, because they both know that the women are worth more. It just shows."

"It's not that at all. It's because if the women get too few there are no children and the tribe dies."

"Well, of course. That just shows again. It shows what men are. You couldn't make a child if you tried. It isn't like making a net or a bone spear. When you think of its hands and its feet and its head, and all its insides, it's a very clever thing to do. I don't suppose you'd even know how to begin."

"Nor would you. I don't think women make them at all. They just grow." At which Elsya was annoyed in turn, because that was true too.

Rita listened to this with amused eyes. Every day she learnt better to understand the differences in their speech, having a clear and vacant mind; but she still used it little herself, for that was the way of the tree-folk—to watch and to understand rather than to change and attempt.

Nor was their speech very easy to her lips, for that af her own people was simpler, and more largely of vowel sounds, which were lengthened and accented in different ways, telling of how they felt rather than what they did, so that it was a better speech for love than for war.

Stele's speech was less simple, having harsher sounds and tricks by which you could alter words when you thought of a past time, so that those who heard you would understand. Rita could use it well enough if the need came, sounding it in a softer way, which Stele, being foolish for all his strength, would be glad to hear.

Rita made no effort to interpose or to speak at all while they debated whether they should go down into the valley of wooden huts. If they had seen her mind they would have known that she thought it such a thing as only cave-men would do, and that because they are half-witted, as was well known, and would always be blundering into some new trouble. But having thrown in her lot with them, she would take what came with a quiet mind.

They did not think to consult her, because they also knew that she was half-witted, having little skill either to speak or plan. They expected her to follow the wiser lead, as the weak and the foolish should.

Yet she saw something that they had missed, had she not touched Elsya with a slow hand on a skin-clad knee. Then they looked at the same thing, and Stele also, and they had puzzled minds.

They saw the beasts move where they fed, on the grassy banks of a stream that ran through the midst of the valley's length, from the high hills to the lake. They did not move as those that change ground of their own will, one after one, with a quiet lifting of heads and a pause to gaze before the feet go forward. Rather, they hastened, not as in any panic of fear, but as being moved by a will behind, so that they bunched somewhat in the rear.

Their distance was great, and they were not huge, like the rhinoceri of the plains, though they were much larger than men, being of about the same height, though they were walking on all their legs; yet when Stele looked with care he could see them well enough, as could the women at his side.

Elsya spoke first, as she most often did.

"They are moving away from a man."

"Girl," said Rita, who had the best sight of the three.

Stele said nothing, for it was a weird thing to watch, and it filled his mind. If they were afraid, why did they not run? If they were not afraid, why did they move away?

He was puzzled, and more curious than before, but he was also afraid of these men who built huts of trees and could move beasts in that way. Because he was ashamed of that fear he rose to his feet and said, "We are going down to those men."

The women made no protest at this, and he led the way at the best pace he could, till he came to a steeper place, and Rita went ahead.

It was late afternoon before they trod grass, and could look upward at those cliffs as at a thing done. Nor would they have done it at all had not Rita been of the three. It was not only that the cliffs fell at a stiff slope, but that they had a surface of shale, of a very brittle kind, so that the little jutting ledges, on which it seemed that a foot might rest or a hand lean, would break off at the first pressure, and even those that held could win little trust. And in places there was no way but by sliding down on a looseness of dust and stone, where it was hard to stop when you would.

Stele and Elsya could climb well, having learnt from childhood what must be done for the meal of a sea-bird's eggs, but Rita was far better than they, having longer arms, and feet that were not clumsy and short-toed, but which could hold almost like a hand, and could close almost in the same way.

Had Elsya shown her mind, she would have been slow to own that there was any girl in the world of fairer form than that one for whom she had made a necklace of pearls, but she looked at Rita's feet and would have hidden her own, had it been a thing she could do.

Rita, who could drop from branch to branch, scarce looking where she fell, but knowing that hand or foot would come at last to a good grasp, was not troubled at all. She would rather go thus than on level ground; but when she saw how clumsy they were, she remembered that they were of a lower kind, and gave help that was quiet and sure.

So they came down by a way that they could not hope to climb again, be the need little or much.

When they stood on grass they were approached by four men who had watched their descent. The men wore clothes of a woven fibre somewhat darker than themselves. They carried wooden spears, but did not lift them as meaning strife. Stele, being one of good sense when he was unvexed and his patience stayed, gave his spear to Elsya to hold, and if his hand was not far from his axe—well, it was the most natural place for it to be, being at the end of his arm. So they met without fear.

The first man said, looking up to Stele who was a head taller than he, "The King will see you at once." The tongue was that to which Stele had been born, though the man did not know how to sound his words as he should, an ignorance which Stele found to be general in that land. Even the King did not seem to know how to speak with a clear sound. Still, it was plain enough. Even Rita could understand much that was said.

Stele answered, "It is for that I came. I am a king's son. I bring a message from king to king."

The man looked at Stele and believed. He said, "It is well. Let us go, for the light fails. Are there more to come?"

Stele said "No" to that.

The man again said, "It is well," and there was more heart in his words. They did not welcome strangers in that land.

CHAPTER XVI.

THE King said, "You come unasked, by a strange way. Can I call it well?"

He sat on the ground, for he was too great a king to sit on a meaner thing than the earth itself, or on one that might let him down, which the earth will not do. He sat on the skin of a striped beast—a beast of prey which he had killed in his youth—that men might not forget the deed.

He sat cross-legged, a lean man, much taller than were most of those who stood round; as tall as Stele, though he would have weighed less. He sat at the back of a triangular hut, of which one side was open to all, and the other two sides joined at his back. All the huts in the valley were built in this shape. They were built according to the shape of the valley itself, which was that of a spearhead, having its point in the hills and its broad base at the lake. Sitting as he did, there could come none to his back, nor to either side.

Before him sat his daughter Tekla, the priestess of the tribe, on his right; and his son Thelmo was on his left.

Before him sat the line of the fighting wives. There were five of these, Amazons, barren and young, who were sure of life while the King lived, but beyond that was a doubt. It would be for Tekla to say that they must die, and if she said nothing of that, it was for Thelmo to say that they should live, which would be saying more. But they had no fear that the King would die. He was still a man of a lean strength, and his teeth were good.

They sat, as their custom was, with their throwing-knives near to their hands. They filled the widening space of the hut from wall to wall. These walls were of the squared trunks of oaks, laid one upon another, and joined with a holding clay, so that they could not be torn apart, even by a great force, this being a secret which the world lost at a later day.

So the King sat very safe, as he knew. For Stele stood before him unarmed, as did Elsya also, and as did the men who had led them. Rita was not there.

Rita sat on the ground about twenty yards away, at one side, so that she could not see the King, nor he her; but she could see Stele and Elsya, who stood without, on the open side of the hut.

There had been some trouble about this, as might be guessed. For, as they came near to the King's hut, the men had said, "You must leave your arms. No one can go to the King's face holding a spear in his hand."

Stele knew in his heart that this was a fair thing, about which one who came in peace should not contend, but he stood silent, being perplexed.

The man saw that he was in some doubt, and added, "You have no cause to fear. We shall leave ours also. It is the custom for all."

Stele said, "With whom?" That was the point of his doubt. Whatever peace they might mean, it might be an easier thing to give the axe to another than to get it back.

In the end it was agreed that Rita should guard his weapons, standing aside. That had been her own thought, which she had given him with her eyes, with which she spoke much.

Now she sat on the ground, and his spear was between her knees. But the axe was in her hand, and should she see that it would be of more use in Stele's, it would be soon there, for she could throw well, as we know.

There was a group of women round her, whom she disliked, but no men, for they stood behind Stele to hear what answer he would make to the King.

The women crowded round Rita, finding her a strange sight, for there were none of the tree-folk in that land. Rita heard their talk, as a man hears the droning of flies. Only, if they came between her and Stele, so that she could not see what he did, she would shift the spear in an idle way, so that they broke somewhat apart, lest they should take a hurt that was not meant.

Stele looked at the King, and he saw a face that was high, narrow, and gaunt, with very piercing eyes. The cheek-bones stood out through the stretched skin; there were many lines at the eye-slit ends, and at the corners of a thin mouth. Youth was far behind, but he saw no weakness of age.

He saw also that the King was not one who could be answered with foolish words. He did not look like a man of war. If he had killed a great beast in his youth (which Stele did not know), he had planned his risk with a cool brain, seeing that there was gain enough to be won. But he was not one who would rule by his club's weight or his spear's craft, as most kings did at that time. He must be met on a different plane.

Stele had the wit to answer with simple words. "You may call it well, for I come in peace from a far land."

"So I saw," said the King. "Are you a son of the Coiling Snake?"

Stele was surprised. How should he know that? Yet it was simple enough. He had said himself that he was a king's son. The King, who knew much, had some knowledge of the coast tribes. He saw the pearls on Elsya's neck. They were a sure sign. He saw other things. He was a man who saw much.

Stele said, "I am the first son of the Coiling Snake, and his daughter also is here." He told the mission on which he came.

The King listened to that. Then he said, "Will you tell me why I should not feed you to my own god and take the girl for myself, making no payment at all?"

Stele said, "Because I offer a better thing."

The King looked as one who would hear all, and judge it with care. "It is not plain that you do."

"Yet I may make it plain," Stele answered to that, not showing the fear that he felt. "For any man may destroy, but a king builds. There are men in my own tribe who do not understand which is the better way, as I found when I would have built them a dam; but you are greater than such as they."

When Stele said this, the King looked at him with more keenness than before, but he was not quick to reply. When he spoke again, he asked a new thing.

"You would be king of your tribe when Coiling Snake dies. If we made friendship now, could you bring them here to my aid if a need rose?"

Stele thought of the men of his tribe, who were fishers and men who lived ever on the seashore. He thought of the long way he had come. He did not think that it would be useful to lie.

"No," he said, "I do not think that I could." Then he added, "But there could be no cause for such aid, for you dwell secure in a strong place."

"You know nothing of that," said the King; "but I can see that you would be of no use to me. As to this plan that you speak, it is of no more use than yourself. It might be good for you, having the custom of which you tell, but our customs are different. I have one daughter, and she is the priestess here, and has a great power. Do you think she would leave it to stoke a sea-cliff fire? "

The King looked at Tekla as he said this, and Stele looked in the same way. She had a dark face that was proud and strong. Two upright spirals of horn rose from her hair. They were the horns of a small deer, and gave grace to her head. She was clothed in alligator skin, very softly tanned, and so made that it was a close sheath to body and limbs. She looked slim, but that was from her height, and because she was so narrowly clad; for she was strongly made, so that she could have broken Elsya across her knee.

Stele looked at her and their eyes met. At the first glance he thought that she approved that which she saw; after which her eyes told him nothing at all. But she spoke, and her words had a plain edge. "Would he call me a fool?" She spoke without anger or heat, as one who puts aside that which is not worth thought.

He answered as well as he might. "Yet my tribe is not small, and it may gain in wealth when I rule, for I am one that would plan. When I left, it was of a total of fifty tens, without counting the unweaned babes or the old that sit in the smoke. If I had such a queen I could do much."

He saw well that Tekla would be something more than a common wife, who would cook and breed and be content to sit and scratch herself in the sun on the fine days, talking to the other women of the troubles of babes or the ways of men. But beyond that, he was puzzled, for he had counted the huts as he came down the mountainside, and they were not more than six tens, and he did not think that more than five could dwell in each, even counting the young, and it might be much less than that. Yet there could be little of human life in the barren hills or in the great lake below, and it seemed that they were a small tribe dwelling apart, for how could men climb the slopes which had been so hard to descend? And the mountains upon the farther side were of a much greater height, rising to icy cliffs of an unscalable kind. Yet he felt that there was something more to be learned. He could not say that he had been received with a great front either of strength or state, and yet there seemed too much head for the tail.

But the King's answer showed that he was unmoved by the boast of fifty tens. "You get no wife here. It is forgotten that you have asked, because it was of a folly that you did not know. As for the girl"—he paused, and looked at Elsya with speculating and appraising eyes—"she will improve, and the pearls are good. Thelmo can have her, if he will; but he will have better wives. It is getting dark now. I will decide these things at the fourth hour from the dawn." He turned to the men who had brought them there, telling them to put them into a vacant hut. He said other things which they

64

did not hear. The men led them away, Rita joining them, and return-ing his weapons to Stele.

They were led to a hut which was newly built, and quite empty inside. Stele looked round it, and was not pleased. He had been thinking as he walked. Now he asked, "Can we have food?"

"You can ask the King at the dawn."

"But we need it now. There may be things I can give which are of more worth."

"The King ordered that you should have no food."

Stele knew that for an ominous thing. But he answered without change of tone: "Then we must look for ourselves. We cannot starve till the dawn. It is not forbidden that we walk abroad?"

"If you steal, you will die. It is the King's word. You are not under his cloak at all."

"But we are free to go?"

The man spread indifferent hands. "You may go where you will, if you steal naught nor cause alarm in the night."

CHAPTER XVII.

IT was getting dark as they stood in the empty hut. They did not stand long, for they had come through a hard day. They sat on the ground.

But they did not turn to sleep, for they were hungry, and they had reason to think.

Elsya, who may have had least to fear, was the most afraid. She was set on flight, so that she forgot how she felt.

"The moon will rise in an hour. When they are all asleep we had better go."

Stele did not deny that, nor agree. He asked, "How? Could you climb back by the way we came?"

"No. But we—there must be some way; we could swim the lake."

"Rita could not swim. The tree-folk never can."

Rita spoke then. "I could go up the hills."

Elsya looked her doubt. "Are you sure?" She remembered the precipitous crags and the loose slopes, where there was no foothold at all. And the hills on the farther side were a harder thing.

Rita was quite sure of that. "I could go up in the dark." She was puzzled in mind that anyone could think of trusting life to a deep lake, which is a treacherous, choking thing, when you might go up the side of a solid hill in the safe air; but she remembered that they were still only people of the caves, though she might have made them her friends.

Stele would have liked to be away, but he was not sure of the wisdom of flight. He wanted to think.

He said, "Anyway, we must sleep first." He was quite sure of the wisdom of that, because they would not have strength for a long flight without any sleep at all, and if they must sleep it was best to do it where there was no fear of pursuit, and while they had not shown what they meant to do. Also, he knew that men sleep most soundly at a later hour, and that it would be foolish to attempt flight at the rise of the moon, sunset being but an hour past.

So they lay close, for at this time of year the valley was hot in the day, but the nights were chilly, when there was an open sky and the wind came up from the southwest, as it did that night; and the women slept, but Stele lay awake, thinking what they should do.

Yet when Elsya waked from an evil dream, the night was far gone, and Stele slept as one having no care. She was trembling from the thing which she had seen in the dream, about which there was nothing new, but when she had thought where she was, and what might come with the dawn, she was in the greater fear, and she shook more than before.

So, at that, she waked Stele with an urgent hand, and he sat up, with a quick grasp on the axe.

"Time to go?" he said, and he made it clear by his tone that he was wroth to lose his sleep in that way. "We are not going at all. I should have waked you if we were."

Elsya's voice shook. "I am afraid of this place. There are dreadful things...."

"You are a little fool," he said, in a worse voice than before. "We shall come through well enough."

It may be that he spoke as he did because he was not sure of the thing he said. He added, after a pause, "Why can't you be quiet, like Rita, and trust to me? She doesn't make scenes in the night."

"She doesn't understand. She isn't like us."

Stele didn't dispute that. Who could? He didn't suppose she understood much of the peril in which they lay. But her arm had been over him when he waked, in a way he had liked to feel.

As to Rita, she had waked at the first movement that Elsya made, though she lay still, as her way was, even leaving her arm where she had not known it to be, till Stele pushed it off as he sat up in his haste.

She lay as though she still slept, but her thought was, as it had been before, that they were a half-witted kind, climbing down into trouble in their clumsy way, and then being surprised at what they found. But she had made them her friends, and would hold their part in her own style, having also a greater confidence in Stele than he had in himself in that hour. Beyond that, she knew that he would not consult her, nor look to her for a wise plan. He would expect her to follow by his rule, if he expected anything of her at all, so that she had the freedom of those who walk in a willing way. She went to sleep quickly enough, but the image that had been in her mind had been of insects that walk on a flower's rim, not knowing that it is closing to make a meal of their struggling limbs, which was a thing she had often seen. For she thought in pictures rather than words, having few of such for the abstract things.

So Stele and Rita slept again till the dawn, and neither knew that their arms went where they would, but Elsya lay on Stele's other side, and there was no more sleep for her.

For there were memories of that which was past, and fears of that which was to come, that entered ever to vex her mind, and would come again if she thrust them forth, moving in a throng which would never cease; and there was not a good one among them. It is a way that the night has. To lie and think in the night is a very foolish thing.

Elsya's hand went to her pearls, and it was a hand that shook, for even they did not feel safe. She feared for them, and she feared almost as much for Stele and Rita, for she was of a loving and generous kind when other feelings allowed, and she had a strong affection for Stele, and Rita was one that she could love with ease. It seemed a natural thing that Rita should love the one man in the world that she could not want for herself.

Elsya feared for them more than they had feared for themselves, and that was not only because she was of the sort that will have grief in the dark hours. She was one who learnt more from the blood's pulse than the spoken word. She had looked at the King, at Thelmo and Tekla, and at the five wives (who were not wives at all in the common use of the word), and her heart had paused, as though she had looked on death. That was before there had been any word from the King.

Now she could think of his words: "She will improve and the pearls are good. Thelmo can have her, if he will, but he will have better wives."

They were hateful words. They may not seem to us to have been so bad in themselves, when we consider that for a man to have many wives was natural to Elsya's mind, but they were discoloured by her aversion to the lips by which they were uttered, and by her hatred of Thelmo, who had done the worst to her that a man could. He had not looked at her at all. His eyes had been for Stele. Elsya could have forgiven a blow, but not that.

She did not mind the idea of being one wife among others. She had seen how it worked. To have only one wife might be best for a man who was the more likely to have peace in his cave, but for the wife it is less sure. It is a harder life, having more toils for the two hands, and it may be of a dull kind. The best life is to be one of several, and to be first of all. That was Elsya's idea, and that she would be first she had little doubt. Next to that, she would be content to be the bride of a prince who would have only one wife, as Coiling Snake had proposed. In fact, she had rather liked the idea. She would be first in a new way.

But now she was not sure that she would be first after any manner at all. She saw herself left alone, her friends dead, herself doing the meaner toils of her husband's hut, bearing blows that came from a woman's hand, which was an evil thought, for a woman's bruises should be made by a man—and she saw her pearls on another neck.

Her teeth closed at the thought, and her hand ceased to shake. It would go hard with that woman. She should die in the night, though it might mean that Elsya would die on the next day. And the pearls should be hidden where they should not be found—they should be cast in the lake. She did not turn her thoughts to ask why she had lost confidence in herself, why she was so moved because an old man had said, "He will have better wives." But the fact is that she was a very frightened girl, and one that was sick for her own home, which had been much to her, though it might seem little to us. She had much confidence in herself, in her smiles, and in the quick skill of her words, and in her coaxing ways, but if this confidence shook, she was a timid thing. She was not made to be bruised. She had learnt to be bold in the sea-depths, for she had sought pearls, which had been a great lure. She had killed Amul, but that had been quickly done, and she had seen at once that there was no other way. Had she thought of it for a night before it had not been so easy a thing.

Now she feared and hated the King. She hated and feared Thelmo also—hating even more than she feared. But she did not hate either of these as she hated Tekla, who (as she thought) had also given her no regard. She did not hate her for that. She hated her because she was of a type of beauty that she had not seen before nor imagined. She did not think that Tekla was more beautiful than herself, but she saw that there might be men who would hold that view, which is as bad if not worse.

She was puzzled by these women, as Stele had been in another way. She had seen the men of the tribe, who were a head shorter than Stele, and she thought them of small account. She had seen some of the women also, those who had been gathered round Rita when they had come away from the King, and most of them were not for envy, but for contempt. There had been some of which there was only one thing to be said: they would make bones in the pot. That was a saying among her own people. If there were one of whom you would say no good, or of whom there was no good to be said, you would say, in the voice of one who would not be unfair to the worst, "Oh, she would make bones for the pot."

So these women had seemed to her in the dusk, but those in the King's hut had been of a different kind. They could not dwell in one place. There were the five who were neither women nor men, as her instinct told, though her mind could not explain. They had been of the same size, of the same style. They had looked to be of the same age. Elsya thought that to pick five who were so alike there must have been a wide choice. Her thoughts turned for a minute's length to think of the basinets they had worn, which had been covered with serpent skin, which was strange to her, and the colours of which, black and yellow and olive-green, were very clear in her mind, as were the aigrettes of parrot-yellow which were on their left sides. She was not sure that she would not like one of those basinets. She thought of it on her black curls, and she was not quite sure. She would like to see how it would look in a clear pool. Of course, she would not wear what they wore. They would be told to wear something else. Then she remembered again. The programme might be somewhat different from that.

Oh, that she were back in her own cave, curled in the corner that she had made her own for a dozen years! Not alone in the cave, which she shared with eight other girls who were too old to dwell in their parents' caves and too young to wed. She had always dreaded to be alone. She liked to lie by herself and to have her own dreams (if they were good, as they mostly were), but she liked to know that others were near.

She was puzzled by those women, and by the King and his son, who were so different from the other men of the tribe. There was a mystery that she could not read. She was afraid; and with the fear came a terror of the loneliness which is the lot of all—has been the lot of a million million of men since the world's dawn. Some lonely thoughts, and a little heap of memories in a skull's space, which are piled up for a time, and then fall apart, having been nothing to others, who have their own—that, and the dark curtains of birth and death that are before and behind, and the unstable beauties of a world in which nothing will cease or last.

So she lay and feared till the dawn came, having those thoughts which come to all, but are told to few. But when the light was very faint in the hut, so that she could not see yet to the farther wall, she rose up so quietly that even Rita did not hear, and went out to see what she could.

CHAPTER XVIII.

THERE was more light outside than there had been in the hut, but it was still very dim, and there was a white mist on the grass, so that she could see but a yard ahead, or it might be two, and she moved slowly and without a sound. She thought more of what she might find than of how she could get back to the hut, which should not be hard when the dawn widened and the mist should clear. She had a purpose in her mind, which was to find the lake, and to see what hope of flight it might give, which she thought to do before men were about; but the real cause that she rose was that she could lie still no more.

She had not been long gone when Stele waked, and Rita at the same time. He was half vexed that she was not there, and looked out, but he saw that she must come back of herself, if at all, for she could not be sought in that mist. He thought her one who could care for herself, and that she would not be gone far. Perhaps she was seeking food. He could understand that. He felt that he could have eaten a cod, leaving neither gills nor tail; and he knew that if Elsya were hungry, it was a more important thing than if a dozen others were in the same state. She was not one of those who may have a slight pain or a mild desire.

He spoke to Rita, Elsya having gone. It made them of a closer intimacy that she was no longer there.

"I think we had better wait here till the mist lifts. I suppose someone will come before long. They cannot mean to keep us ever without food. It cannot be scarce with them. They do not look like men who labour overmuch, or who go short. I did not think it wise to try to escape in the night. There may be traps set. Had they not known that we could not go, they had not left us thus in an open hut; that is, they had not left us so unless their own thoughts were peace, in which case we had put ourselves, perhaps, in a needless peril and in a foolish wrong."

Rita thought that was sense, though she was as hungry as he, and it was a newer feeling to her, for she had not known it till the last days, there being always food in the trees. There was food in the caves too, but it was of a less regular coming, and there had been times when it fell short.

But the light got more and the mist cleared from the upper air, so that they could see the mountain heights when they looked out from the hut, though it still lay low, and they could not see far over the grass, and Elsya did not come back.

After a time the man came who had been their guide to the King. He came as one not seeking speech, but that he might see that they were there as he passed, as one counting his stock. When he saw there were only two, he came to a pause.

"There should be three here."

"She is not far," Stele answered. "She has gone round the hut. The mist hides."

The man would have gone on, seeming content with the reply, but Stele stood in his way.

"Do you not feed your guests in this land? We have not even water to drink. Shall we lick grass?"

The man said, "But you are not guests. How can we give food till we know the King's will?"

"Then can we go forth?"

"By what way?" The man seemed amused.

"If we cannot go forth, we must have food here. Would you force us to take, that there may be cause of wrath?"

"There is milk enough," said the man. "You can take what you will, but we may not give. There will be no quarrel for that. You may milk the mares—if you can." He seemed amused again. He went on.

Stele had not seen a horse, but he understood the milking of goats.

He said to Rita (for he was of the kind who cannot think well without speech), "These must be the great beasts that we saw from the mountain-top. We have goats on the sea-cliffs with whom the women make friends. Sometimes we kill their young, which are good to eat when they have been scorched at the fire. After that the dams are glad to have their milk drawn, which the women do, making more for our own babes, so that we gain all along."

It seemed a good way to Stele, of which a man might boast, having got the best of the goats by a cunning wile; but whatever Rita may have thought she said nothing. He had reminded her that he was a man of the caves, which she was more glad to forget.

her own choice." The King thought that he saw far into his daughter's mind, but he was still unsure that he saw all, in which he was right, as he most often was. "We will say no more at this time." He left Thelmo alone.

Thelmo thought for himself. He was not foolish at all, though in this thing he may seem as one whom his sister ruled, the fight being hers at the root, and one that she must win by a lonely path, if at all. He remembered that she had said that she did not care which would be first. Perhaps she might have meant that which she said.

He could not tell what his sister would do, for in the depth of his mind he did not think that she meant that either Stele or Elsya should go to her god; but he could not see how she could get clear of that, having made the claim which so many heard, or how she could bring her own wish to a good end even then, for her father had said that Stele was not one that he would have, and he would not easily change from a fixed mind.

Thelmo saw that he must leave these doubts till he could talk with her again. For the next thing, he would do well to talk to his coming bride, for though she might be his only for a month (or two, if he would), which he was slow to think, yet there was much that she would have to know, as would Stele also, and he was the one that should tell. So he went his way to the hut to which the three had returned, and where there had been talk enough before he came, as it would be easy to guess.

They were content, in the main, with the way that the thing had gone, as it would look to any from their side that they had reason to be; but they were puzzled as to what Tekla might have meant at the last: "I claim them both for the god." They would return to this again and again, being that which they could not solve.

Stele said, "It must be some protection by which we are made safe in the tribe, or some rite by which we are made of a high caste; for what else could it be? It is the same for both, and she would not mean aught but good for her brother's bride."

Elsya said, "It is more than that. It is something which we do not guess, and which I have a heart to fear. Yet I am not greatly afraid. I am less afraid than I think."

This was shrewdly put. Her mind was drawn in different ways by two things which she had felt, and which were more to her than a reasoned word. On the one side, she had not liked the sound which the people made when they had heard that they were claimed for the god. It was something that she could not fit with the ideas which seemed good to Stele, and so she put them away. But on the other side, she was quite sure that Thelmo wished her no ill, and she was

as sure that he and Tekla were of a common will, so she turned the
doubt from her door.

She did this with the greater ease because she had much else of
which to think. She had formed a sure thought that Thelmo was
prince of a larger place than this valley, and she was eager to know
of what she would be queen at the last; she wished also to know if
he had other wives, or if she would be first in time, as she meant to
be in other ways. Then she was curious to know what might be the
marriage customs of a strange land, and if there would be some rite
in the gathering of many eyes, as she would like it to be; and she had
a girl's thoughts, which have been alike at all times, for her clothes,
though it may be for no more than the bliss of a ringed nose or a
feathered head. She had no more than her pearls and the dusty skins
that she wore; and Rita could be of no help, for she wore nothing at
all. Nor had Rita any care for such customs as these, for, had she
talked of them at all, she would have called them of a vulgar kind.
She would have said that if two would mate, it was for themselves
alone, and there could be no time at which others could be better
away.

But Rita had her own thoughts, which were the trouble of one
who comes near to the grasp of a sought thing and is not sure what it
may prove to be. At the sight of Stele she had come down from the
trees, seeking a strange love, and had found it hers, and she was told
now that Elsya would be left here, and that they two could go back
to his own tribe, at what leisure they would, and she could see that
he was glad at the thought.

Doubtless he would expect that she would be his in the quiet
woods, and that they would go back to dwell in his cave, and to take
rule of the tribe when Coiling Snake should be dead. She knew that
love is more than a tale of two who lie close in a shadowed place,
and she was afraid of how at last it would be. For she had no heart
for the caves, nor for the ways of those who could live such lives,
eating fish that their hands had killed or that had gasped to death on
the shore. She was not quick at their speech, nor did she wear their
skins. She did not like the way in which they would ever be doing
things for which there was no need, when they might lie stretched in
the sun and be aware of themselves; and the smoke of their fires was
a very filthy thing.

She would have been very glad to be back in the dear home in
the trees, where her birth had been, but she knew that she would go
on, from step to step, never turning at all, and yet dreading what the
next would be. So she had grief at a joy which might be less near

than she thought, which had been a grief of another depth had she known what the doubt was.

But Stele felt that it was all near to a good end.

He was confirmed in this when men came bringing more food than they could eat in a week, asking if it were as they would, and going with quick feet for such kinds as Rita would be more glad to have. Nor was it of a different face when Thelmo came to the door, saying that he had much to tell, and might he eat with them on the same floor? Which they were pleased for him to do.

CHAPTER XXV.

THELMO drew Stele to talk of himself for a time, for he would know more of this man whom his sister sought. Stele told of how he should have fought Borl, and of the mischance by which that was stayed. "So I have killed none," he said, in a modest way, "that is, of our own kind, though I must be near to my full strength, and may be chief of my tribe even as I sit here." (For they sat round the spread food on the hut floor as they talked.) "I should say that you have done more, having had, it may be, better chances than mine."

Thelmo, who was little older than he, allowed that might be no more than truth. "At least, if you call them equal to men, which we scarcely do. I have killed many of those who come through the great swamp, but there was little merit in that, for the battle lasted three days, giving time for much."

"That was far from this vale?"

"It is of that I would tell, among many things. For, after three days' time"—he turned to Elsya as he said this—"we must go to that land." He did not say that they must return in a month's time if his sister's claim of themselves were to come to its due end.

Elsya was glad at that. Her eyes shone, and she looked at Thelmo in a way that he would learn to love, as she meant that he should. "My heart knew well that you were a greater prince than of this vale."

Thelmo went on, seeing no reason to guard his speech, for these were things that his wife must learn were she his for a week or a life; and whether Stele went by the secret road to the end which the King had meant, or whether he went to his sister's god at a later day, it mattered not what he heard or knew. It mattered only that he should have no fear of guile, such as might be passed over to Elsya's mind. And if things should come to another end, and Tekla should have her way by a means that he could not guess—well, then he must come to this knowledge too, so it might be said to both, and the time was saved.

94

"The way out of this valley is through the hills on the eastern side. It is not over the hills, which will never be climbed by man on that side, as you can see for yourselves, but by caverns that none may trace (except that the way be shown), so that they die in the dark; for there is no light by that way."

"You will tell me," Stele said, "if I ask that which were better left, and I will take it in the right way; but I would know why you hold this valley as so secret a thing, your father being king of a greater land on the other side of the hills."

"It is a thing that would be asked by any," Thelmo replied; "yet it is simple enough. The valley is known to none, for the lake, being of three miles' length, and twisting somewhat among the hills, closes its mouth, and the beasts that are in the lake are such that no man would swim by that way, even though he could swim so far, and had hope to find aught for his toil. We keep secret that which we have found because we can withdraw when we will, either for counsel or rest, and the people of my father's land see no more than that we enter the mountainside, bringing, it may be, no food nor aught else for our need, and we are within (as they think) for many days, and come forth as we were, having communed with gods. It has a simple sound, yet it makes our rule sure."

"That is well to know, and it is a secret that I shall keep very still in my mind, both for the oath that I shall swear, and for Elsya's sake, that she shall ever have this sure place to which to flee if she must. But there is one further thing that I would ask, and then I am done. I would know what your sister meant when she said that we were claimed for her god."

Thelmo may not have liked to be asked on this point, but he met it in the best way that he could, giving as much truth as he dared, which he judged to be better than a made tale.

"As to that you will soon know, for you will see him in three nights from now, if it be a sight which you choose. You will say that it is no god at all, being no more than one of the beasts of the lake which has grown too fat to go free; but it is not to be said in a loud voice, for to the valley-folk, it is a great god. Now that you have been claimed for the god, the people will bring you all that you can ask to have, as you have already seen."

"Why should it be seen," Elsya asked, "in three days' time, and not now?" She did not like the sound of what this god was, and she would learn more.

Thelmo must go on by the path that he had started to take, and he trod it so that it was less bad than he had feared it would be. "You need not see it then, but of your own choice. I gave you that time because we have one that is doomed to die on that day for a good cause, and he will be given to it for the food it needs."

"I hope," Stele answered to that—and the smile with which he spoke was more of the lips than the heart—"that your sister would not claim us for a like end."

Thelmo gave an answer which was frank enough, and Stele was inclined to believe that he meant all that he said. "My sister has not told me her mind, which she might not thank me to guess. She would rather show it herself in her own time. Yet I think she meant no ill, neither to yourself nor to your sister, whom I shall wed, for you will see that you are both in the level cast of that net."

"I am sure alike," Elsya said to that, "that she meant us no ill."

"I am of the same mind," said Stele. "Yet you will see that it had the look of a spear which might point the wrong way."

CHAPTER XXVI.

THELMO went on after that to talk of his own land on the far side of the hills, which, as he told it, was of a great expanse, being a fertile plain with low hills at the north, where it was many miles in width, though it narrowed toward the south; but at the east, being the farther side, the ground was flat and low, and sank till it was no more than a swampy marsh, with islands of bushy growths standing up here and there, and this swamp closed in on the south till it met the hills; for the lake which closed the valley in which they were was drained by a river which ran south and then east through a gorge in the hills; it had rapid falls, and then spread out in the marshy lands till it was lost in the swamp.

On this fertile land there dwelt a great people who had been there for more years than a man could count, and had grown so numerous that there had been seven tens of tens of tens at the last count, all men and women in their best years, for the old and the children had not been counted at all.

There were old tales that if any could cross the swamp they would come to a land that had no limit at all, very fertile, but being full of serpents and great beasts that it would be terror to see; but no one knew the truth of this, for the swamp had not been crossed in the time of any who now lived, as they were at ceaseless war with those that dwelt therein, and no man unless he were riding a swift horse could go near it and live.

At that point he must stop to tell that the horses, of which they had seen something, were not kept in the outer plain to milk and eat only, but that men would ride on their backs, which was a strange thing to be heard; and when that talk had ceased, Stele asked, "Are there more of the men of the swampy lands, or are they better-weaponed or of a fiercer kind, that they hold you in as they do?"

"They are not men at all," Thelmo answered, "or they could not dwell in that place. They are, as we call them, the Thlantus, the great rats of the marsh."

"I know the Ogpurs," Stele answered, "which are men, though of a loathsome kind, dwelling in holes that they have made in the ground; but of the Thlantus I had not heard. What are they in size and shape?"

"They are like in shape to the rats which may be found in a stream's bank or in the roots of an old tree, but much larger, being half the size of a man, and at times more than that. Also, they are slimmer and lither than rats, having long, thin heads with many narrow, needle-pointed teeth, showing from jaws that are slit far back."

He went on to tell of their colour, which was dull white, of a fish-like look, and how their blood, though it was not reptile-cold, was not of the bright heat of a man's, but ran slow in a chill stream.

Yet (he said) it must not be thought that they were dull of movement or tame of mood because their blood flowed thus in a chill stream from a slow heart, which is easy to understand. For even the reptiles have an agility which is not for contempt, as when the lizards streak from stone to stone. There is no slowness in the sweep of a crocodile's tail. But these were not reptiles. They were mammals of the swamp, animals with keen brains in narrow heads behind their hell-red eyes, animals that bred too fast for the feeding that the swamps supplied; that gluttoned ever in thought upon the root-rich fields of the plains that the men tilled; that had a fiercer thirst to suck the hot pulses of one that they had pulled down, while he yet lived. Animals of an age that had not yet bent its neck to the dominion of man, that yet fought for freedom if not for supremacy in a lawless world.

Furtive and fierce, they lurked along the edges of the swamp, restless ever to cross the ten-mile barrier of a plain that was kept barren to part the swamps from the fertile lands and the dwellings of men. They were scarcely checked by the knowledge that those who ventured first would very surely die, whatever might be the fate of others that came behind.

Elsya spoke at that point. She was of fickle moods since she had known what her fate would be. At times she was shy and glad, and she had sudden fears and quick beatings of heart, so that she thought that those round her must hear. Ever she watched that Thelmo's eyes should come her way, though she would not always look back when they did. She was jealous of the talk that went on, though it was for her that he spoke, and she did not hear more than half that was said, though it was so much to her gain to know.

But she heard this talk of the swamp-rat's teeth, and she said, in a quick fear, "I will not go to that land. Thelmo can have me here if he will. There would be no rest, neither by night nor by day."

Thelmo did not look pleased at this. He did not wish that he should marry a coward. Yet he looked at her, and could not feel as wroth as he should. He thought that she might be one of those who will do more than they boast, which showed that he was wise for his years.

He answered, without heat, "You need not fear to come, for the Thlantus would never reach to the strong place where we should dwell, nor am I one with whom a wife would be less than safe at a need. I would not have you to think that. Beside, you are wrong when you think that there could be no peace either by night or day, for they cannot see in the dark. They are then more sightless than we. On the moonless nights the patrols are called in, and we sleep in a sure peace."

"Have they never crossed the barrier-plain," Stele asked, "so that they have done harm to your fields?"

"They came often at one time in small bands, doing much harm at first to the crops, and then taking children and horses as their boldness grew.

"At that time we relied only on a barrier fence and mound which we had built round the whole land on those sides, from which watchers looked over the plain.

"Then there was a time when they came in a force that no man could count, and were met midway on the plain in a great fight, in which more than half of our people were slain. That was before I was born.

"After that we began to train the horses to carry men, and with them we patrolled the plain through the daylight hours, hunting down any that came out from the edge of the swamp.

"When I was a child it was hard to get men to ride on these patrols, for though they might kill many, their own end was ever the same. It was said that they would never live more than two years. For you must see that, there being so many miles to patrol, they must ride alone, or in parties of few, if all points were to be watched at once.

"Then my father made the Amazons, who had been before but a king's guard, into a larger force, giving this work to them, which has been well done from that day.

"It is they whom my sister leads, they being known as the Left Wing, for such they are when the whole army moves out, the horses being fed in the meadows of the north, where the land is most wide.

"Yet there are more of the rats (or so it seems to us) every year, and they have been very bold of late. It was last year that they came out in all their force, as they did in the earlier time, and it was a three-days' fight that we had before they were back in their own place. At that time we were only saved by those of the Left Wing, who rode through them from side to side till their horses could do no more."

Stele asked, "What are they whom your sister leads? Are they women or men?"

"They are not men," he answered, "nor are they women, though once they were; for my father made it a law that every year we shall choose twenty of the best of our girls of the fourteenth year (or it may be more than that, if there have been many losses that should be replaced), and they are cut with stones, as was done before to those only who would be of the King's guard, so that they will bear no babies to their lives' ends.

"After that, for five years they are trained in riding and in the ways of war. Then they must take their turn to patrol the plain at its farther side on the swamp's edge, being ten miles from the dwellings of men. They know that they will be pulled down at the last, feeling the swamp-rats' teeth tearing at throat and thigh, and they count ever the tale of deaths they give before that evil shall be."

"Yet I see not why they should go ever childless before their deaths."

"There are good reasons enough. Would they ride at peril ever with minds that are fierce and free, had they babes in a left hut?"

"Yet it is strange, if you would have your race grow, that you should thus deal with your women, from whom its increase comes. Could you not better spare a regiment of men of a like kind?"

"It is a thing that we could not fail to ask of ourselves. But the answer is that a sexless man becomes spiritless and heavy of flesh. He is slow to move, with little courage to fight, though he may be spiteful more than enough; but a sexless woman, being in her strong youth, is of another kind, being without pity and without fear. She is like a fierce cat that would let no other life endure, her own being cut off as it is."

Stele was silent for a moment after this had been told, and then asked, as one in a doubt who would not say the wrong thing, "Yet, unless I err—and I speak as one who would be told if he should ask that which should be left unsaid—your sister seems not of this kind?"

"My sister," Thelmo answered, "is as she was born. She leads the Left Wing of her own choice, having a great hatred of the Thlantus, as I have also, which may be from this root, that it was but two months before our birth that a troop of them found their way to the

100

place where our mother was, and she held them off till help came, killing two with a spear of bronze."

Elsya was somewhat bored by this talk, which was not of those things that she was most eager to know, yet she would not be rude to Thelmo, nor win the rebuke of Stele, who would not care what he said. "All this," she said, "is a tale to hear; yet I would know most of the ways of life in your own walls, and of what houses you have."

So Thelmo turned the talk to strong houses of wood, and herds of goats, and garments woven of hair, and of pits for the tanning of skins, and of the tin and copper which were found in the northern hills, which could be blended to a metal of stubborn strength, and of a bright dye which could be made from a plant that grew in the swamps, and of cunning workers in bone and wood—of all which Elsya was glad to hear, thinking that she would be queen in a great land.

But Rita listened to all this, saying nothing at all. Her thought was, "Why do men come down from the trees, which are safe and clean, to find this trouble and dirt?" But it went on to show her that she was doing this thing herself, though (as we can see) she knew the voice of the serpent for what it was.

CHAPTER XXVII.

TEKLA took Elsya to her own hut, that she might tell her the marriage rites and find her what she might wear.

She gave her a pair of deer's horns for her hair, and showed her how to fasten them on. They were of a straight spiral, not more than five inches long, bone white and well polished, making her hair more black than it was before.

"It is god's luck," Tekla said, "that I have any such here, but of seemly clothes there is nothing that can be found in this savage place. For at this time you should be clothed in skin of lizard or snake. You should be covered from neck to knee, that none may see what you will give to him that you will wed, and it should be a covering that fits close, that all may envy what it will be. There is nothing of such kind in this vale. Yet you cannot be wed in those skins, which are of an old filth, such as would not be easy to cleanse."

She looked at her own tunic of white, which she wore only in her own hut while she was here. Elsya tried it over her head. She was lost in its width, and it fell near to her feet.

She laughed at that, looking up at Tekla, who was more than a head taller than she. She said, "You must be of a great strength."

"Thelmo is stronger than me, though we are of a like height. You will learn his strength when you are wed."

"It is a good thought."

Elsya would have gone on talking of Thelmo or of herself, which she was ever willing to do, but Tekla held to her point. "It is large, yet it must serve."

Elsya said, "That is soon changed. Give me threads, and a good needle of bone, and I have my own knife with which to cut. I will make it to fit well. Tell me what I shall say and do."

"There is not much that can be said or done in this place. It had been different in our own land. We shall gather the people in one crowd, that all may see. Then you will go up to the King, who will stand, and you will kneel at his feet and say in a clear voice, 'King, I would wed your son, if you will.'

"And the King will say, 'Will you be his, to take his babes in your womb, or his spear in your heart's depth?' And you will answer to that, 'I will be his, to do as he will.'

"The King will say, 'You will be none but his while you both live?' And you will answer, 'I will be none other's at all.'

"Then the King will turn to Thelmo, who will be standing at his right hand, and will say, 'Son, here is a wife of a good kind.'

"To that Thelmo can answer in two ways. He can say, 'She is dirt to me,' and the crowd will laugh, and you will go where you can; or he can say, 'I am in want of a wife,' after which he will stoop and lift you from where you kneel, and carry you to his own hut, after which you will both do as you please."

Tekla said this over a second time, that it might be learnt well, but Elsya was not one to forget. She considered it, and was not over-pleased. She said, "It is not worth a high price. Does Thelmo promise nothing at all? Yet it matters naught. Men will have their words, but it is a woman's way in the end."

"It is more than words," Tekla answered, "as you should know. Were we in our own land when a prince is wed, it is custom that a faithless wife shall die in the bride's sight of a cut throat, and such may be kept alive for a long space, so that she may serve her use on the right day. But these people of the vale are a dull folk, and I doubt that there will be one such to be found."

Elsya yawned at that. She did not greatly care—as her mood was at that time—whose throat might be cut, so that it were not hers. She laughed at a new thought.

"When you wed," she said, "you will have a small choice. There are few who could carry you in that manner. I hope his hut will be near."

She would have said more, but she stopped at the sudden anger in Tekla's eyes. She saw that which she had not guessed, though she was quick to judge, both of women and men. For a second's space she saw, not a woman friend, but the fierce, implacable eyes of the priestess of the valley-god, of the Leader of the Left Wing, and they were not easy to meet. She would see that glance once again, when they were to look their last at one another in a place of death and high deeds; but they would not know that at this day. In a moment it had passed, and Tekla said, "I am a king's daughter. I should not wed in that style."

"As to that," Elsya answered, boldly enough, "I am a king's daughter too. Is this a marriage that does me shame?"

"Yes, I suppose you are. There is no shame at all. Thelmo will wed you with all the honour he may. But you have not seen our land."

Elsya might have left it at that, but she was one who was not easily still with her tongue. She went on: "You might wed Stele and do well. He would carry you for a mile, if there were such a need, though I think you are little shorter than he. He carried Rita for half a day, hanging down his back like a dead deer, though he was sulky about her weight."

Tekla looked at her with attentive eyes, which were now under control of a strong will. "What is this tree-woman to him?"

"She is nothing as yet. She follows him as a child follows those to whom it looks for its food, but she holds off, as one dreading a seen end."

"Yet they sleep in the same hut. They lie close at night on the same skins. He may do as he will."

Elsya wondered how she should know this. She said, "You are wrong in that. He will never do as he wills. It is she who will bend that bough."

Elsya did not know that she had said ill, but there was little but cold speech between them after that, at least at that time.

The next day Tekla was as kind as before.

CHAPTER XXVIII.

THE wedding was as Tekla had said it would be, and there is no need to tell it again. Elsya said her words without fault, being too nervous to fail. She meant them as much, or as little, as women do at such times. They were incantation rather than vow. She had a little dread, in the dark rear of her mind, that Thelmo should change his will, and should call her dirt to her shame, and she had a sure faith all the time that he would say a different thing, as he did.

She knew that she looked her best, as there were eyes enough to behold, though she would have had them more. She wished much that those of her own tribe had been there to see.

In the end Thelmo picked her up, and carried her off with an ease at which she was well pleased. She said, as he put her down in his hut, "You could carry two such as I. You should have wed two, being so strong." She scarcely knew what she said, for her heart beat very fast, and she was more frightened than she had thought to be.

She said, "I am not to be hurt!" for she was ever a coward at pain. She had heard tales of what may be when a girl comes first to a man's power, and she was much smaller than he. After that she had moods. She pleaded. She teased. She mocked, "Will you never take me at all?" But at last she kissed hard. Thelmo was well content. He knew that he had a wife of a good kind. He thought that they would do much, being together in days to be. He thought little of his sister's claim. He said, "When you see my land you will know that you are to be a great queen at the last. It may be that you will be the greatest that the world holds, when we have conquered the swamp, as I have hope to do."

It was a foolish boast, for no man knows of the days to be, and those who guess will guess wrong. But they slept well for that night, and Elsya waked with a glad heart, and must tempt him that he would love her again, which he was very ready to do.

CHAPTER XXIX.

IT was that night that Stele and Rita came to the same end, though by a different path.

For they were alone in the hut when the night closed, and it was different now that Elsya was gone—as they both felt, though it would have been hard to put it to speech—and they had come to a strong love, and were in their first youth and in vigour of life. Nature cares nothing for the mummering of men, nor for a priest's prayer, nor overmuch for a man's joy or a woman's pain. She plays for a new life. Next to that, for a safe nest, where it may grow. And it was the doubt of this last which had held Rita back for so long. Now she put that doubt from her mind, seeing the way she must tread; and having come to that point there was no cloud to her joy. For she was different from Elsya, being of braver heart, and thinking less of herself. Also, though of the same years, she was much older of soul, having had a more leisured life, and thought much as she had sat in the summer sun, when she had been tired of play, or when she had lain close at her mother's side, in the dark of the colder days, going little abroad unless the sun showed, but staying in the high shelter that they had built, and eating at times from the food which they had stored in a tree's gap, yet feeling little of the cold, for her fur was thick at that time of the year, falling off in the spring, till that which remained was little more than a fine down, as it was now.

So having come to this mind, she let Stele know that he might do as he would, which was very quickly done. She did not love after Elsya's way, being without fear or guile, but Stele saw no cause to complain. They went their own way (as they thought), and Nature had hers, which (as we have said) is ever for the living babe—and even one that is weak is a hope, and so is better than none. There are those who dream that they can do better than this, and that life may come to a safe end by a fenced way, being unstrengthened by any strife, which may be true when the stars fail.

But there were four who waked at that dawn, each having a glad heart; and there was one who waked alone, having no joy, to brood plans in a doubtful mind.

CHAPTER XXX.

IT was the night of the next day. The moon rose early in the southern sky, being two days on the wane. It was a moon of more brilliance than is ours, except in the tropic lands, and on that night there would come a time when it would shine straight down through a fissure in the rocky hills, piercing inward through the high side of a great cave, and moving down its black wall, till it fell at last upon the blacker water of a still pool, which was in the midst of the cave.

It could have been seen at that time, by one whose eyes had become used to the dark, that the sides of the pool were high and steep, but having a stair cut in the rock which led down to a narrow beach running round the pool, between it and the steep sides.

The cave was large, with a wide level of space round three sides of the pool, and it could have been seen in the faint light that it was crowded with men. All the men of the valley were in that space, and the women too, except such as had babes to watch, and the King was there, seated on the ground, as he ever was, and Thelmo sat before him on his right hand, and Elsya on his left, and before them was the Amazon guard; but Tekla stood in another place.

She was clothed in the reptile-skin which she ever wore in the sight of the valley-folk. On her forehead, between the horns of deer, there was a large and luminous stone, the like of which is not now in the hands or knowledge of men, though such may be found again in the deep hills, when a man shall go far enough in the right way. Also, she had a knife in her hand.

It could be seen by the stone's light (for the moon did not shine on that side) that a man stood before her, and that his hands were bound at his back. There was none that stood, beside these two. All others sat on the ground; among whom were Rita and Stele. Rita watched all with a thoughtful mind, wondering much at the ways of the men who had left the trees. Stele watched as closely as she, and with less ease of mind than he would have liked to have, being alert to see the ways of this god to whom he had been given without his will.

Elsya watched too with a curious mind, for she was ever one who would see all, but there was no fear in her heart now that she and Thelmo were one. She felt that she had come to a safe place.

They stood silent and still, Tekla and the bound man, till the moon's light fell on the dark pool, and there was a stir from its depths. Then Tekla spoke to the man.

"You know the law. If you answer that which I ask, and do that which I say, the god may eat or spare; but if you delay either to speak or do, you will be thrown in, bound as you are. How came you here for a god's meal?"

"I am condemned thus," the man answered, "because I thought to follow you through the dark caves, which is against the will of the god."

"Are you the first to try this wrong thing?"

"I am the third."

"Where are the two?"

"They have both gone to the god." The man's voice shook as he said this, with a fear that he could not rule.

"You have spoken truth. I will loose your hands, and you must go down the steps at the best speed you can. It is death to be slow in that. When the moon moves from the pool you can come up if you still live, for the god will have granted your life."

The man turned, and she cut the rope from his hands. He ran down the steep steps, which were roughly hewn in the rock, and having no rail, with such haste that he was likely to have fallen to the water below, and so ended at once. Yet he was barely in time to save meeting the god at the stair's foot, for he came from the centre of the pool with a swift rush as he saw the man on the steps. Meeting at the water's edge, the man dodged the beast, making a swift turn, and ran round the side of the pool. With a bark of anger the beast gave chase, showing himself, as he came clear of the water, to be much larger than those that swam in the lake. It was through that size that he was fast in the pool, for when he was young he had found a way from the lake that was under the water's height, and had gone out and in till he grew too big, and so here he was to his life's end.

To Elsya's eyes he was slow and fat compared to the one she had seen before, and it seemed to her in the pale light that his body was covered with swellings or cysts of an evil growth, but it might have been that they were but fungi of a foul kind that had taken root on his scales.

Fat though he might be, he waddled round the pool's edge at such a speed that the man must break into a rapid trot to keep ahead of the hungry jaws that snapped at his buttocks' height. Yet he might have kept ahead with no worse than a panting of breath till the light moved from the pool and he was free to go back by the way he came, had the margin of the pool been of an equal width for its whole girth. But there was one place where it was no more than a foot's width, and this narrow path was not flat, as was the most of that narrow beach, but shelved so sharply down that a man must move with slow feet, holding to the side of the rock, lest he fall into the depth of the pool.

If the reptile were close behind when the man came to this place he was no better than dead, for it could plunge into the lake and swim up to where he clung with one stroke of the tail, and pull him off by the leg, but if it were well behind, his chance to cross might be good enough. For if it should take to the water from where it then was, thinking to catch him up before he had gone far, he could turn back, and run past in the opposite way, and it would have all its trouble to begin as it had been at the first.

Elsya watched this play, as the man circled the pool three or four times and was still uncaught, and she liked it well. She was not cruel of heart, but there was no cause that she should care for the life of a man that she did not know, and he one who had proved to be of a spying kind, against the will of her friends. She wondered whether there had been any who had come back up the steps as the light failed; and when there was something that she would know she had a tongue that was not easily stilled.

She said to Thelmo, "May we talk in this place?"

She spoke in a low voice, aware of the soundless hush that had been in that crowd since the moon came, and Thelmo answered in the same way. "You may talk, if you choose words."

If they spoke low they could not be heard but by the Amazons who sat at their front, and by his father the King; but he knew, if she were incautious of words, that she might say things that were not good for his father's ears.

She said, "Doth no one escape? Saw you that? It was a close thing."

He answered, "There was one only who came near to saving his life. He had very active legs, and, at the first, he could leap the gap, but he lost strength at the end, and failed at the last round."

Her eyes wandered to Tekla, who stood where she had been at the first, the knife still in her hand, and her face lit by the stone she wore. It gave to it a cold blue light, as though frozen to a like stone.

She looked down on the man, but not as caring that the god should have his meal, but as one whose mind was on farther and very sombre things.

Elsya asked, "Is this custom hers? Or was it of older time?" She did not think of the foul beast as a god, and she saw well enough that it was a device to end those who were better dead; also she knew that women are by nature more cruel than men, though they may whisper a different tale in a man's ear; yet it did not seem such a sport as Tekla would have thought for herself. Thelmo answered that with a free tongue, knowing that there was none of the valley-folk that could hear his words. "It is older than she. There was a priest here when we came first who had been told by the god that no woman should rear more than three babes, and those she had beyond three should be fattened for him to eat in the third year. Also the old, and those who were maimed by mischance, went the same way.

"My father asked him if he were sure that such was the god's desire, and he said that if the god were of a different mind it would surely be shown, for he would not touch any who should be thrown to him against his will. He said this where all the people could hear, and my father said that the god's will should be obeyed.

"But the next night my father had a dream in which the god came to him wrapped in a red flame, and in wrathful mood, saying that the priest was too old, and that it was time that he should come to his jaws, as did others of the same age. The King told this dream when all were gathered on the next day, and the priest said that the dream was not from the god at all. My father said that this might be true, but it seemed to him that it was a thing to test, and that it was such a test as could do no harm, for (as the priest had said) if it were not the god's will, he would not take him at all. But the god took him from the very foot of the steps with an eager snap, so that the people saw that my father's dream had come from the right place."

Elsya laughed at that. It was a good tale. Thelmo went on: "The god ate the priest where he pulled him down at the pool's edge, and sank back into the lake at last, leaving no more than a picked bone, and my father said that it was the god's will that who should be the first to go down the steps and stand at the water's edge should be in the priest's place, if he should show that such was his pleasure by letting him go free. Tekla went down the steps, and stood for a time at the water's edge, but the god did not rise at all, and she has been priestess from that day.

"After that the god told her that he was getting tired of the flesh of men, and most tired of those who were old and tough, or who were too young to have any flavour, wherefore he would only eat men from that day that were of the middle years, and when the light should be on the pool as it now is.

"The people were not sorry for that. The mothers, and those who were in their later years, took it for a good word. Yet they asked, 'What shall we then do when the children grow in numbers and size and the old men are slow to die, and the valley becomes too arrow for the life it holds?' The King said to that, 'Every winter I will take half the children of the second year, and though they pass to another land, and their mothers will not see them again, yet they will grow to a good end.'"

Thelmo might have said more, but he saw that Elsya had ceased to heed, for the play came to its last scene. The man came to the narrow place, and the god was close at his heels. He tried a new feint, turning and leaping back, so that he passed over the eager jaws, but he could do no more than come down on the beast's head, where he sat, facing its tail, and spreading his legs apart, so that they should be clear of the teeth.

The god shook his head with a sudden jerk, but the man would not come off, for which he cannot be blamed, at which the god jumped into the pool. There was a great splash and a cry, and then the pool became still, except for the slow circles that spread for a time from where the struggle had been.

Thelmo said, "That is how it always is at the last. There is really little to see."

CHAPTER XXXI.

TEKLA knew that a man may have more than one wife, though a woman may not act quite in the same way. There are good reasons for that, as a child may see. A man may wed with four or five wives, and his children may be five times as many as one would bear, but a woman cannot increase hers in the same way. Though a man have many wives, it will bring no doubt of who may be the parents of every child; but if a woman act in a like way, she will have children of whom the father may not be known but to her own mind, and it may be not even to her.

Even if all that be put to the side, Tekla had no cause for wrath that Stele had met a woman of the trees while he had been unknown to herself, and had taken her for his use, as she supposed that he had. But the nature of men or of women changes little as the ages pass (if it change at all, which would not be easy to show), though it may be that in the world's dawn there were men of strong limbs and of heavy jaws who were gentler than are we of a later time, as it is natural for strength to be, and as we may see it today in the gorillas that would live at peace, but that men have killed for the mere sport of seeing a dead thing.

Tekla looked for a mate, as a woman should. She saw Stele as one of a better kind than were most of those of her own land, and one whom she would rather wed than that she should be under a man of her own race who was of less rank than herself. It was a chance to take with a quick hand. She would not deal at his price, which was to leave all that she was and had, to pick shellfish on a barren coast, and to sit in a smoky cave, but she would have him to deal at her mart, and to pay the price that she set. She had his life in her hand.

As to wives, he could have all that he would, either first or last. She had no thought to make the world in a new way. But she would be first of these, as a thing of course, being that which she was. With a woman of her own race who would be slow to see this, which was a slender chance at the most, she would know how to deal. But this tree-woman was of a different kind. She knew that in their animal way (being scarcely to be counted as men) they would mate for life, and would have but one, being in this (as she had heard it said) as stupid as the wild geese, who may be slow to mate anew, even when they do no more than think of a dead thing. What her custom was might be little to Stele—who was of another breed—in which there would have been hope but that she had seen the looks in the eyes of those two, which she did not like.

She knew that she held power in her hands. She could order the woman's death. She could let Stele know that his life was to be saved, if at all, by her own wit. She had a fierce desire for him in her heart, and she had power in her hands. That should have been enough for most. But she was of a great pride. She had been ever slow either to bargain or beg, which might have mattered less, things being as they were, but that she was one who would reach her end by a clean path, which it might not be easy to do. Then she had the King's will to thwart, and there was the claim she had made which covered not only Stele, but her who was now her brother's wife.

She passed Thelmo as they came out from the cave, and he saw that she was of a vexed mood, which is easy to understand. Seeing that, trouble stirred in his own mind, for she had Elsya's life in her hands by her own plot, and Elsya was more to him by a night's play than he had thought a woman could be.

He said to her, speaking apart, "Goes it well?" And when she did not answer to that, "I cannot walk in the dark. I must know all." She looked at him with startled eyes, as one made awake by his last word. She said, "There is nothing that can divide us two." It was no answer to that he had asked, but he understood. He said, after a pause, "That would be true at the last." He waited for her to say more.

When she spoke again, she went wide of what was in the minds of both, as she had done before.

"There is an old shrine in the northern hills. It was built by men who are not of our time. It is broken now."

"Yes," he said. "I know it well. What of that?"

"It was the shrine of a god."

"So it was," he replied. "But it is nothing now. You cannot read the god's name. It is but graven marks, which mean nothing to us. He is no more than a dead thing."

"Yes," she said. "So he is. Even gods die."

He thought at first that she spoke only from such mood as will come to all at times, showing life as a futile thing; but he thought after that she had offered words, as she sometimes would, having more meaning than their surface showed. Gods might die. If a god should die, it must end a claim that had been destined to fill his jaws.

"Would you that?" he said, with a new hope.

"Would I what? We have but talked of a dead shrine. I have said nothing at. all."

After a time she added, "I know not what I will. That is plain truth. But you may sleep in peace, Elsya and you."

CHAPTER XXXII.

RITA talked with Stele at the same time. He had not liked that which he had seen, and he felt that there were hidden things that it would be well to know. Rita thought to the same end, but there was less hidden from her, because she searched by another road. She felt that she was in a pit of filth, but she was there at the call of love. If Stele's life were at stake, she would fight to the most she could. She would not be weak or slow, as she had shown more than once in the past days. But she did not choose to walk by that road. Why had he come down from the hills? Yet here they were; and she was his, as she thought, to her life's end by what had been in the last night, and she must learn to walk where he would.

Tekla had judged her well enough, as she had looked at her over the pool's breadth, seeming to see naught. "She is one who would harm none, being left in peace; but she would fight for her mate if the need were, being neither weakling nor fool." So she thought, and beyond that, she could admire a grace of form that was almost of her own height, though of lighter build, and the golden down that lay so smooth and close, which few might be found who would praise at this day on a woman's back. She thought only that she was too long in the arms, as Elsya had thought before.

Stele told his doubts, fearing that the King would bring him to death, though Elsya might be left alone, being his son's wife. Rita could say naught of the King's mind, but of Tekla she spoke as of a seen thing: "She does not know what she would. She is in a great doubt. Yet we shall be safe enough, if the last word be with her."

"Well," Stele said, "we can but watch as yet, and be ready for all. Tomorrow it seems that we shall go to the new land, when I suppose that we may have better hope of escape." He thought Elsya safe, and his only thought was to get back to his own tribe by the shortest road he could find.

CHAPTER XXXIII.

THE next morning at the first hour of the full light, Elsya came to the hut where Stele and Rita were. She had a message from Thelmo. It said that they should stay in the hut (except at the King's call) until they should hear again either from Tekla or him.

Elsya added to this, "We are to start at noon, but about you two there have been some words between Tekla and the King, who wished that you should stay here. She gave way when she saw that his will was fixed, but Thelmo says that the game is not played to its end."

"There is something hidden in this which I do not like," Stele said. "We are treated as guests in this place. We are well fed. We may walk as we will. Yet there is no friendship shown. If we are to go free, as the King pledged, it would seem that now is the time, when those of his own house are to leave by the secret way. If we are to stay here, I must think that he means us no good. Can you not ask Thelmo that he shall talk in a plain way? "

Elsya said, "I have done that in the last hour. I said I was ill at ease, having seen the ways of the god whose I am claimed to be, and more so if you be held here. He said I was at his side in a high tree to which no evil could climb. I said I would take no comfort in that if you two were yet on the ground; to which he said, 'Would you cry a wound, having a whole skin? Let it be.' And after that he gave me the message which I now bring."

"Then we will wait here. You will not go without coming to us again?"

Elsya promised this, and her word held. It was an hour to noon when she came again. She was in a blithe mood, and began to talk before she had shut the door of the hut.

"There have been things to see! Yet I will tell you the end first, though I thought we should not reach it at all, so that you can hear with quiet minds. You are to come. That might not have been, but that—but I must begin at the right end."

"The end may be the best place," Stele struck in, "if we are to start at noon. You must make a short tale."

"It shall be short enough. There were valley-men that would speak to the King. He received them as he did us, and I was there, being who I now am, seated at Thelmo's side.

"It was that man with the hairy face, and the voice that squeaks when he talks fast, who spoke for the rest. There were three others with him, and all the people seemed to be there, standing back, but not too far to hear what was said.

"The man talked for a long time, very fast, and saying the same things three or four times, and the King listened and said nothing at all.

"The man stopped at last. He had only said one thing all the time. They wanted to know the way out of the valley, so that they could go in and out as they would, and see what became of the children that the King took every year.

"Then the King said, 'Have you quite done?' He did not seem angered or in any haste. He went on: 'Did you show me the way by which I come, or did I find it myself? It is mine to keep or to give. It is yours to find if you can. Yet I will give thought to this thing you ask, and answer you when I next come, which will be in three weeks from now, for we go for no more than a short time. As to the children, would you have them thrown to the god, as they once were?' The man said 'No' to that, and the King asked if they would have them stay in the vale till there was no food for their mouths. The man said 'No' again, but they would know how they fared, and would see for themselves. He got bolder because the King spoke in a mild voice, and at last he called in a high, squeaking way, speaking very fast, that they would have an answer now rather than when the King came again. The King said, 'Do you threaten because I have had patience to hear you talk?' The man said 'No' again, but that they were many who asked, and they would have an answer while they met in that way.

"The King said, still in a quiet voice, 'You are many and we are few. That has the sound of a threat. It is a word which I will not hear.' I did not see that he made any sign as he said this, I being somewhat forward and sideways from where he sat, and how could it have been seen, they being seated before us, as they were? But she of the Amazons who sat in the midst drew a knife from her belt and threw. It was so quick that; there was no motion of any till the knife was in the man's throat. It went in under his chin, and must have gone deep, for he fell down, and scarcely moved where he lay.

118

"The King looked at the man who stood next to him that had fallen. He said, 'Take out the knife. He had squeaked more than enough. I would see him bleed.' The man did not move, seeming struck with fear, and the King said, 'Would you all die? There are knives that wait. You will take it out, and cleanse it on your own cloth, and give it back to her to whom it belongs.' At which the man stooped in a shaking haste and did what he was told. After that the King said, 'Now you will take him, you three, and no others shall do this. You shall hang him on the best tree that grows in the place where your huts are, and hang him so that all may look and think well.' So they began to do this, being still in the range of the knives, which they might well fear, and as they picked up the man the crowd broke up, murmuring among themselves, but with no heart to do more.

"This was but ten minutes ago, and as the crowd broke Tekla looked at the King, saying, 'Would you still have them to stay here?' The King said, 'They must take their chance. They should come to no harm. They are aside.' Tekla answered, 'I meant not that.' The King looked at her in the slow, thinking way that he has. He smiled at her, and she at him. They seem good friends, even when they fight with their wills. He said, 'You could say more than you do.' She said, 'So I will. If they would be loyal to our part, and have no doubt of aught that we may plan, you or I, then it is no harm that they come; if they are not loyal, and would take a chance to do us what evil they may, would you leave them here? Would you give a leader to this scum?' After that we spoke apart, Thelmo and Tekla and I, and Tekla said that I should take no heed of that which I might have heard, but that I should tell you to be at the caves' mouth at noon if you would be free of this vale."

Stele said, "There is no need for words, but we may think as we will." What he thought was that the King must have meant him ill when he had refused him leave to go forth, and it seemed that Tekla was a true friend. Yet it was Tekla who had claimed them for the god, which was that which would not leave his mind. He resolved to go forth with open eyes and a ready spear.

CHAPTER XXXIV.

RITA stood in the dim light of the cave-mouth, and looked into the black hollow ahead. It was a fearful thing to go under the mountains thus, where one might be crushed or lost in the black night. Very fearful to one who had been born in an open place. Elsya could not feel as she, nor could Stele help her in this, for they had been born in a cave. They would think that the farther a cave went into the dark hills, the more safe it would be. She knew that she must draw together all the courage she had, as a man draws round his body a cloak which is of a scant size. She did not think that she was bound to go by this way. She had a thought that she could climb back by the way they came if she were alone to do as she would, with no other of whom to think. She was less than sure that she could not find a way over the great heights beneath which they were now to go. But where Stele went she would go too. Nor could she tell a fear which would be foolish to them. She took her place on the chain.

This chain was of hammered bronze, very hard and strong, having been made of much copper and little tin. It was a long chain, having hanging loops of metal at distances of three or four feet, large enough to take a man's arm. Tekla took her place at the head of this chain. She was dressed as she had been when she had given food to the god, wearing the luminous stone on her forehead, between the horns. They had no other light than this. Elsya went next to her, and then Thelmo, and then the King. After that there were two servants of the King, of whom we have not heard, they having no place in this tale; and then Rita and Stele, and the five Amazons in the rear. Stele did not like the place that was his, for he thought with truth that, if the King had spoken to her who went behind to put a knife in his back in a dark place, she would do it with a good will; yet what could he do? They let him bring his weapons without a word said. He had a thought that they would not do him wrong where Elsya could see or hear. He must take the chance.

Each of them put a left arm through his own loop. They went through the god's cave to its darker side. They climbed rough steps in the rock. They went through a narrow place into another cave which may have been very large, for they could not see to its sides, having no light at all but that of the stone which Tekla wore. Yet she led them on at a quick pace, not keeping to the wall of the cave, but crossing its open space as one who walks a known way.

Then they were in a passage, if such it could be called, having a side that shelved over their heads from the left and a floor that sloped away from beneath their feet, and there were times when there was wall on their right hand so that they must squeeze through a narrow space, and at others there was no wall on that side, either to feel or see. Those who walked at the tail end of the chain had no light at all. They walked in the black dark, and there were times when a word would be called back that they must step with care in a place of rocks, or that they must make a great stride where a fissure yawned, and they would drag in the chain as they moved slowly with feeling feet.

Stele thought, "Why do we walk in the dark? There could be torches made from the pines on the hill-slopes. I have seen lamps in their huts which are not of a bad kind, though they should be carried with care." He saw that it must be so that the way should be a very secret thing, even to those who were brought in the King's train. Yet, he thought, it has been found in the past; it is known of some. He knew that he had a mind that could judge nicely of space and turn. He counted steps; he watched for gaps in the wall. He listened when water fell, that he might know at which side it was, and how far. He learnt much, yet when they came to the third halt, and it may have been night by then, for they had come far—but who could tell? —and there was talk that they were near the end, he knew that there would be little chance that he could find aught but a cold death in the hollow hills should he venture a lone way, either to return or to come again.

The third halt was in a place of caves, many and small, and here there were lamps to light, and store of food and of other things, and beds for rest.

There was a tunnel beyond these caves, at which a watch was set of an Amazon at its black mouth. Not that there was any fear of attack, but because, when the dawn came, there would be a point of light at its farther end, and then must all be roused. For when the King went into the hills it was his custom ever to come back at the dawn.

CHAPTER XXXV.

IN the place to which they had come there were stores kept in the caves. There were clothes and other things which were used in the valley, but not in the wider land; there were others which were laid aside when they entered the hills and taken up when they went forth.

For when they entered the hills, it was thought of all in the King's lands that he went to commune with the high gods. He must go forth as he went in, with dress unsoiled and unchanged, as must his children and those who went with him (but not, as it was said, into the holiest place).

Tekla would be no priestess when she went forth, nor would she wear the lizard skin in which she had sat at the King's side when we saw her first.

She changed now (after she had taken some sleep) into the garb of war which she wore when she rode on the barren plain, chasing the rats back to their native swamps. This was made of the tanned skin of their own bellies, soft and tough, and of a grey colour, and was ornamented, or armed, with fringe and collar of their own teeth, needle-sharp, and so placed that they would give greeting to snout and paw in a grappling fight. She covered herself thus from head to heel, for it would be her first deed, when she went forth, to ride with the next patrols, and to see that there had been no fault of guard during her absent days. But as yet she went with her head bare.

And being now ready to go forth at any time when the word should be called, and having that on her mind which would not wait, she went to speak to the King, whose rest (being an old man and a lean) was soon done, and who was as ready as she.

"Father," Tekla said, "I would talk."

"It is time," said the King.

"Our wills have not been at one, which is not well between such as we."

The King smiled as one unmoved, though in a kind way. "My will has been at ease, walking a vacant path. "

Tekla did not like that. She thought that her father held her at something less than her true worth, yet she saw that the event might seem to equal his word.

"Let that be as it may. I am of a changed mind."

"So I saw," said the King.

"Yet I do not say you were right. We may both have been less than that. There is a third way."

"There is ever a third way."

Tekla was annoyed again. Would he have her think that he read her mind to its depth? She fenced with an equal skill. "Is it good?"

The King did not answer quickly to that. He knew as well as she that there were more than three ways. He guessed what was in her head less surely than he would show. "It may be good enough. Let us have plain words."

"It was for that I am here. When these strangers stood at your door I thought them to be of a good kind. I said in my heart, 'Here is the man I will wed.' I looked next at the girl, and I thought, 'She is good, though in another way. Here is Thelmo's mate.' When Stele gave the message of Coiling Snake, it had a good sound, except that I should go to his sea-cliffs, which was vain, for they knew not how much we are. That I refused. Yet I thought, 'When he sees all he will stay.' I had been at ease as to that, but I saw you had other plans."

"Daughter," said the King, "I saw all that you say. I would have given your wish with a glad hand, but you saw not the fruit which it would be like to bear. It had been folly and wrong."

"Let that be as it may, for it is no more than a dead dream. I am of a changed mind. I wed none. Yet you were wrong as to the girl. I will say that to the last. She is of a good kind. She must be Thelmo's wife to the end."

"I have the same thought," said the King. "Yet two may come to the same spot walking by separate ways. Why do you say that? I told you that she is of timid moods and of a jealous sort. Are these good in a king's wife?"

"She is one who would fight hard for her own. Had she babes to guard, she would bite as a cat bites. She would be wakeful to watch their lair. These are good things in a queen. Also, she is very true to her friends."

"You have seen well," said the King. "But I have seen farther than that. She shall come out of this place as of a high birth, being more than woman or man. Do not all know that we commune with gods when we come here? They have given Thelmo a bride. She will be more than any that he could take to wife from our own folk. Her children will be a race apart, and the rule be sure to a far day. There is but one thing to be faced. Why did you claim them both for your god?"

"As to that," Tekla said, "I may have been right or wrong. Yet I am the priestess, and there is none that can change my word. It is between me and the god. If we are at one that she live, you need not trouble for that. You can leave that to me."

The King mused for a time. He could see trouble of a likely kind; so, he supposed, could she.

"Yes," he said, "so I will. Have you more to say?"

"Yes," she answered, "as you know well enough. We must talk of Stele."

"We may talk till we tire," the King said, "but it will not change that which you can see if you will. The man must die in a quick way, and the woman beside, you having been stubborn to bring them here. For if we have it thought that Elsya comes from the gods, there must be none who may tell truth in a simpler word. Had you wed him it would have brought evil at a far day, but to turn him loose to live, having no bond, were a nearer risk."

"He would have the bond of his sister's good."

"It is not enough."

"Yet we must find a way. They shall not die at this time."

"Daughter," said the King, "I will be more frank than you. There is that in your heart which I do not read. I saw that you were of a changed mind, yet I saw not why. If you have no longer a will for this man, why would you guard his life at your land's risk?"

"Father," she answered, "I will show my mind as a skinned skull. I will be second to none, Should he wed me, he would think first of the tree-woman, who has few words but who sees all.

"I am not one who can be bought at that price. I have seen myself in these days, and I do not boast. I am one that will die with a barren womb rather than bend with a hurt pride. It is more than sorrow to know; yet, being said, it sounds but a mean thing."

"Let it all be as you say," said the King, "yet you itch at a flea's bite. The woman were soon sped. You could have the man as you will, were there no trouble but that."

"There is another thing which I have learned in the last days. I cannot walk by that path. It were joy enough to see the blood run and the life go from her eyes, yet it were but a short joy, and there were a long grief for a thing which I could not change."

"It would seem that you can read all, even yourself, which few can. Yet I had thought you to be of a less meek kind. I had not thought that you would let this tree-woman have a full meal while you thirst as you do."

"I had been of the same mind but a week back, and I walk now on a thin edge. I have seen my knife in her neck, from a good throw. I have seen it in her loins, so that she would die by a slow way. I have led her to where she would fall by the swamp-rats' teeth. I have seen her jump at the snap of the god's jaws. I have thought of new deaths. That is how I am, and how you think me to be. Yet you must think beyond that. I was born of two. I have thoughts which war with these thoughts. They cannot cause them to die, yet they can make them too weak to be changed to a wrought deed."

The King was silent at this, for it was a true word that she was born of two. Her mother had been a great queen in ways other than his, giving her life for the tribe at a sore need, in a way which he would have been slow to do, and yet of so weal; a heart that she could not hate her foes as a woman should. There was a door in his mind that moved as Tekla spoke, so that the hinge creaked, but he closed it with a firm will. It is not good to think of a dead past, having fallen to smaller days; nor of a dead love, having no more than that which is bought with beads.

He said, "Let all this be as it may, yet they must die for the land's good."

Tekla had a subtle thought, which was not of her mother's blood. She asked only, "When?"

"As to that," said the King, "it is to be so done that Elsya shall neither know it nor guess. They shall be sent with gifts as to their own land, being told that they must speak no word of what they have seen, nor come ever again. Elsya will care little for that. What is a brother to one who is newly wed? Stele will buy his life at what price he must. They will go with a guide, that they fall not to the swamp-rats' teeth; but a guide 'may leave in the night.' He will leave when the path turns at the lake's edge."

"It is a good plan," she said; "yet it is one that I have seen better than you. When the gods of the hill-caves give Thelmo a bride, do they give her a brother also, and a woman of the forest-land?"

The King was silent at this, stroking his chin. He said at last, "I will not change my will that they die, I yet I will hear what you would say."

"It is simple wile, and one that we may spread out on the floor where we all sit. We can speak our thoughts without hiding or lies, and they will see that we plan well. Elsya will go out with us alone.

It is that she be of the gods, which will please her enough. Stele and Rita will go back to the vale, having been seen by none but those who are with us, who will not speak. You can tell them that they can leave later in a quiet way, but not now. Elsya can go back to the vale on a near day, and she will see that her brother is well. After that you must do as you will."

"So," said the King, "you win his life for a time." He saw well what she would do, yet he could not deny that it was the better way.

CHAPTER XXXVI.

TEKLA sought Stele, who was with Rita in a cave by themselves.

Being roused, they rose up from a bed.

There was little of her mother's mood in Tekla's heart, seeing them thus. She thought that, had she had Rita alone at that hour, she would have killed with a quick hand. Rita saw this well enough. Saying little, she saw much. It was of her kind that she saw more of the moods and meanings of men than of the things which they did, or which lay at their hands.

She was less fierce than Tekla to hate, and, besides, it was she who won. But she saw the peril in which she stood, and which might be Stele's. She had thought much of ways in which she might guard her life at need, since she had come down from the sure peace of the trees. Even Tekla might not have found her easy to kill. But it was not to be tried at this time.

Tekla looked at Stele, and her mood was not that of which she had told in her father's cave. Had she been asked did she hate or love, would she slay or save, it had been hard to say. Had he not made his choice of a woman whose skin was covered with hair, who was too long in the arms, whose feet would curve like a hand? And not in such choice as that of a man who would gather wives that he may be great in a tribe, having many young, but as of one to be at his side, both in the night and the day. So she saw, for love had been thus since the world's dawn, as it will still be when a thousand races have bared or blackened the land and have found their end, and the earth is green again with a new hope.

On his part Stele looked to her to speak, with a doubtful mind that was far from ease. He was alert, as one fearing a trap.

He was not of the kind which will dream a peril which is not there. He was not of those who dream, but of those who build. It was for that that Coiling Snake had seen that he would make a good king. A man may dream a roof first, having no props, and it is no difference at all. He may add the props when he will. But they who build will find that there is a price to pay for that which is left unthought, though it be but a wooden peg.

Stele had thought much as he lay, putting sleep aside, for he was strong both of body and mind; but he moved ever in mist. He could not come to a clear light. He did not think that harm was meant to Elsya, and Tekla's claim had been for her, as for him. He thought Thelmo to be of a straight speech. Of Tekla he was less sure. As to the King, he would not trust him the length of a man's stride, and it was of him that he was most greatly afraid. So far he saw clearly enough, but he could not tell what it all meant, nor (which was the cause that he had lain awake in the night) could he be sure what it were best to do. He watched now as a wrestler stands await for one whom he would let try for the first throw.

Tekla said, "I have been at speech with the King. We are near to come out to the light, and to our own land."

Stele said, "It will be much to see."

Tekla thought, "It will be much to him. Will it aid him to see that I am more than this beast of the trees? He will see much that he has not thought to be—not in his life's length. But he will see naught if he go back now." She had a doubt that her plan was less good than she had thought it at first. Yet it was good for the time, and after that it might be changed.

She went on: "The King hath a good plan. It will make Elsya more than a queen-to-be. She will be goddess as from this day. She comes out from the hills where the gods dwell. They have given Thelmo a bride."

Stele said, "Elsya will fit that part as a kernel fits to a shell. She could strut well from her birth, or, at least, at the next spring."

"But there is more to hear. A goddess comes not forth with a brother and woman of the tree-folk."

Stele saw that with ease. Her brother would be god too, which would be little to the King's mind. Was the peril near? He said, "But the plan was that we go our own way. I have no will to stay here. It is a pledged thing, and it will fit this plan as a knuckle fits to the joint."

"So it was," Tekla answered, "and so it shall be at the last, but not yet. For the time, the King wills that you shall go back to the valley-folk."

"I see well," Stele said to that, "that we should not come out with you to the light; yet I see not that we might not wait till the dark, and be led forth and away, so that none should heed. It were soon done and the shorter risk."

"You see not that, because you talk of that of which you know naught. There is ever guard at the cave-mouth. It must be planned with care. For the time, you must go back."

"For what time?" Stele asked, having no love of this plan. "Shall I not know how my sister fares and if she be in the honour of which you tell?"

Tekla thought, "She will show him how great we are." Why should she not go back to the valley in a short space? They could come and go when they would. They were planned to return at the next moon, before the feast of the god. She said, "Elsya shall come herself before many days, and you will hear the honour to which she wins." She had a new thought. "You can come near to the cave-mouth. You can see the land. You will give word that you go not out to the light. Those who stand in the dark may be unseen, though they see far."

Stele said no more; for what was there to say? The plan had a good sound, but he was unsure as before.

Rita said nothing from first to last. She felt baffled and heavy at heart, having hoped to win clear of these folk that she did not love, nor they her.

It was at this time that there was a cry from the one who watched. There was a point of light at the cave-mouth, showing that the dawn came.

CHAPTER XXXVII.

THE cave-mouth was at some height from the land over which it looked. It must have been a hard way to climb at the first, but now steps had been built in a bow's shape, curving outward from side to side, shallow and broad, and being three tens and four to the count.

Stele did not count these steps, as he would have been likely to do, for he could not come so forward as that. In fact, he could not come forward enough to see very much, for the cave's roof ended, and the darkness therefore, at a place where the rock slit upward in a fissure very narrow and high, so that those who went forth must walk by not more than two, with the walls pressing on either hand.

There was one that had gone ahead at a quick pace to make it known that the King came. Now he walked forward alone. The cave had narrowed as it rose, becoming an upward slit in the rock, very lofty, before it split to the sky. Standing back in the dark mouth, there was not space for a level front. Some must keep to a dark rear.

Elsya walked three paces behind the King. Thelmo and Tekla followed, being side by side.

Elsya saw things which were so strange that she had no eyes for the steps, though they were wonder enough, being of hand-smoothed stone, and showing the labour of many men. But below the steps were horses in ordered lines, to a number of two hundred, or more than that, and on the back of each there sat a warrior, woman or man, of the dress of those who were the five wives of the King. Elsya had not thought that a man could find seat on a horse's back, nor that it could be so ruled to a rider's will. She saw that she had come to a land that was strange and great. If she were to be first in this land, it seemed to her to be no more than a natural end.

When the King had said some words which she did not follow as well as she would have liked to do, being phrased in an old way, with some that were not in her tongue, he called her that she should step to his side, and so she came with a mind that was proud and cool, looking with a smile at those who shouted to greet their prince's bride that came thus from the gods.

Elsya could see more now than she had done while she stood back. There were men who stood on foot round the cave-mouth, on the outcurving platform above the steps. There were others on foot beyond the mounted force. But there were not many of these, for none knew at what dawn the King would come forth, when he went in to the god, and none had thought that Thelmo would find a bride in the sacred place.

Thelmo and Tekla came outward now, and were greeted with a new cry.

Tekla said to Elsya, "I will show you the skill of those whom I lead."

Elsya asked, "Are they women or men?"

"They are neither women nor men. They will breed never at all. They will ride thus till they die with a rat's teeth at the throat. They are the Riders of the Left Wing." She went down the steps, having said this, and one brought her a horse which looked to be of a savage kind, for men held it with ropes, pulling different ways, and looking fearful of that they did. Yet Elsya saw that she walked to it without fear, casting the ropes off, and heeding not that she was in reach of its teeth, and then climbed to its back in a quick way. It was a yellow stallion, swift and strong as it was savage and huge. Tekla rode to the centre of the space at the steps' foot, and gave a call, at which the regiment broke into two parts and rode outward, curving apart, and coming back by such a way that they were face to face below the place where Elsya stood between Thelmo and the King.

They rode now in lines of ten, the horses of each line being of the same colour, black or yellow, or brown or grey, by which they could the more quickly regain their form if they should be scattered apart.

The horses showed their own colours on back and head, but they were all covered below, which was to guard them from those they were trained to meet.

Their legs were cased in reptile-skin, which was smooth and supple and strong, and their bellies were covered in the same way, to guard them from the swamp-rats' teeth. Their manes and tails were clipped close for the same need. Their belly-guards were fastened with girths of leather, drawn over the shoulders and loins, and to these girths there were attached sheaths and thongs for throwing-knives and spears, and for what else their riders might will.

These rode without saddles and with their legs drawn up, so that heel and buttock met, holding on with their knees, which must have been hard to learn; but for those who must watch ever for a rat's leap it was a good way. They looked small as they rode, the stallions being of a great size, and the close-fitting snake-skin showing them to be as small as they were, but they looked lithe and fierce, and it was to be seen how they were trained when their leader gave a sudden cry, at which those in the hinder lines on either hand drew each a throwing-knife with a quick wench, and spun it through the air, so that it was caught by the one of the front for whom it was meant.

This was more than a vain trick, for each Amazon carried six of the knives very near to her hands (being trained to throw both with the left and the right), and each of these was a sure death to one within twenty yards, or it might be more, against whom it should come; and by this means the knives could be passed forward with speed, if those of the front rank should be used and the need last. Four times Tekla called, using different words either for left or right, and twice the knives were thrown forward, and twice returned to those from whom they had come, as the two squadrons swept round again at their highest speed and halted before the King.

Stele saw something of this, as Tekla had hoped that he might, though not much. He had a view of a narrow width of the farther land, seeing buildings of hewn logs, larger than the huts of the valley-folk, and squared spaces of land where but one thing grew, showing that these men had so ruled the earth that it did their will like a beaten child. He saw enough to know that Elsya had come to be queen of a great race, such as he had not thought that the world held, and he had done half of that for which he had set forth. He saw also that he had asked a vain thing when he had thought to take Tekla back to be his queen in the coast caves. Yet he did not think that Coiling Snake would be well pleased when he should take Rita back for the same end, having come from the trees, which he could not hide if he would. He saw that their lives would be hard to join, and he knew not how they would rule their days, whose ways and food were not one. Yet it was a doubt that he meant to bring to a good end, let him but get clear of this trap in which they were caught. He did not think of Tekla at all, except as one who had power which she might use to injure or aid. Had he done so he would have felt, if he had not thought, that she was one who knew too much that he did not, and who would go her own way more than a wife should. As to which he might have seen that there was wider space in some ways between Rita and him, but there was the blindness, or at least the impulse, of love to lessen or leap that gap.

So Elsya went on to be called goddess and Prince's wife by those who lived in a rich way, such as she had not thought to be when she had threaded pearls in her own cave. She lay in a soft bed in a raftered room; she had food of many kinds when she would; she saw things round her of which others must tell her the use, for she did not know her own needs till they were shown; and she took to all with as much ease as a chicken shows at its first drink, lifting her head in the same way. She lay in Thelmo's arms in the night, and thought that she had come to a good place, not seeing farther than that, as few would.

But Tekla rode to the barren plain which lay between the tamed land and the endless swamps where the rats bred. There was talk among those of the Left Wing that the rats were bolder and more at the swamp's edge than had been known of late years, and she shortened their hours of rest, and added two riders to each patrol, for it was their honour to see that the rats should keep to the swamp, or that they should die in a quick way, so that the land rested in peace.

Stele and Rita turned back, to be led again through the long night of the caves. They were guided by one that was most in the King's trust, and who spake no words to them but such as he had been told to do, or which were little comfort to hear. They did not go back at once—resting for a time, and taking food in the caves, as they had done in the night before; and it was at this time that Stele, who looked ever to learn all that he might, noticed that there was a break in the wall of the cave in which they ate the meal, long and low, as it were a level rift in the rock.

He said to their guide, "Is that a hole that ends, or does it go through to a farther cave?"

The guide took a torch from where it burned in a socket on the wall. He held it low. They looked in, seeing some way, but not to an end. There were bones on the floor of this low slit in the rock, about six feet in. Stele said, "What are they?"

The guide said, "They are the bones of one who was lost in the caves, and who tried to crawl through to this place, which (as you can see) it is too low to do. If one shall try to come here from the valley, having no guide, there are many ways by which he may go wrong, but the most will lead at least to a cave which is not more than two tens of feet from where we now stand, yet from which there is no way through but by this shallow slit. If you look through it, as far as the light shows, you will see that it is of so little height that you will wonder that any should have come so far as he did. It is thought that he had been starved till he was so thin that he thought that he could wriggle through, yet he was stuck tight when he was as near as you see."

Stele said nothing to that, though he had more fear of the caves than before. He thought to watch well as they went back, knowing that he could remember much.

Rita said no more than he, but she had more horror than she had felt before since she had followed Stele in the ways of the lower men. To be held so by the rock that you could scarce breathe, nor move forward nor back! To struggle vainly, being so pressed by the rock, which would yield nothing at all. It would be to go mad while you yet lived. It was a horror to think. When would she be again in the free light, instead of here, with the mountains above her head?

They went back after that, following the long path in the dark (but the guide, being alone, bore a torch, so that Stele saw more than he had done before), and they spoke little either to their guide or to each other till they were once more in the sun's light. The guide gave the King's word to the valley-folk, and the word of their priestess, of whom they had a like dread, that they should be treated well, and so they stayed there for some days, doing well enough, but longing ever for some way by which they could go free.

CHAPTER XXXVIII.

TEN days later Elsya came.

She came alone, a very different Elsya from her who had come down the cliffs in the skins, filthy and torn, which she had worn since she left her cave.

She had the short deer's horns in her hair which were sign of rank, and she had on a garment such as Stele had not seen till that day, woven of a plant's fibre, and stained red with an insect's juice. But the necklace of pearls was still round her neck, and looked to have found its place with the newer things.

She had things to tell, many and strange, and the greatest (not to Stele, but to her) was of pins of bone for the hair, which were so made that it could be lifted to certain shapes which were strange to see, but not easy to do for oneself with unpractised hands, so that, for this time, she had left her hair as it was.

As to why she had come alone she was not over-clear; but it had not been meant at the first. It had been the King's will that Thelmo and Tekla should come also, and he himself, but there had been sudden talk of a gathering of rats in the swamp, and Tekla had said that she could not leave till she had seen for herself what it might mean. The King had said that she was right to stay, but Elsya must go, as had been planned, because of some tale they had made that she was going back (for some days) to the gods from whom she had come, and they were in the mesh of their own lie.

Tekla, for some reason which Elsya could not tell, and concerning which Thelmo had been less easy to read than he mostly was, had been unwilling that the King should go if she were held back; and after many words, which Elsya did not hear, it had been agreed that she and Thelmo should come first, and that the King and Tekla should follow when the rats were stilled, which Tekla thought to be a short thing.

Then, at the last, when they were in the cave-mouth, Thelmo had been called back, the menace of the rats (which Elsya thought to have more heed than it should) being said to be more great than had been thought, and so she had started alone, with Thelmo's promise that he would come to her arms again in a space of four days, at the most, or she back where she had been.

That seemed well enough till the four days passed, and became eight, and Thelmo did not come, nor any word through the caves; and Elsya, who had little patience to wait, would walk ever backward and forth in a doubt that was plain to the valley-folk, till Stele said, "Will you never stay in one place? Do you not see that you are watched, and that these people, who are no friends at heart, and who are prisoned here as are we ourselves, can see that something is wrong? Do you take no heed that they are of slower feet than they were when we call for aught, though they have no quarrel with us?"

Elsya said, "Yes, I can see that. I can see more, which is why I fret as I do. There are words said which are not for us. I think they plot some evil, though it may be in a clumsy way, for they are fools, as I think. Yet I would that Thelmo were here, or one other who could lead us clear of this trap."

"Yet," said Stele, "things will be as they are though you walk for a whole day. Can you not sit still in one place?"

"I have no mind to that, whether I could do it or no. I go out in the dark. I will learn more if I can. What can you learn doing naught here? "

Stele thought her a restless fool, for he was one to sit still while in doubt, though he could move quickly enough on a clear path; but in this she was wiser than he, as he was able to see when she roused him and Rita in the darkness before the dawn with a whispered tale of that she had learnt by going on quiet feet.

It was not warm at that hour. Elsya's hand was shaking and cold when she touched Stele in the night, and she was fearful of that she had learnt, but yet of a better heart than she knew, for she had done well, and would have the praise that she loved.

She said, "I have that to tell which should be spoken low; and besides, I am cold. I would lie close to Rita and you."

"You may lie as close as you will," Stele answered, "and speak as low, but I would have it in few words, the hour being as it is. It is time for sleep, not for talk."

Elsya was not pleased at that. "You shall have few words, as you will. The way through the caves is changed, so that those who come to us, as they think, will fall into the god's pool."

Stele was roused. "How learnt you that? If it be true we have more foes than we know, or we are lost in a quarrel which is not ours."

Elsya said, "It matters not how it was learnt. So it is. Few words are best in the night."

Stele saw how she was vexed, but so was he. He would not give her the praise she sought, nor ask more, being answered thus. He said, "So they are. Be it as it may it will keep till the dawn." After a time he saw that there was some fault on his side, and would have asked more, but then Elsya slept, having been awake all the night till then, and come to a warm place. Stele thought, "It may be more tale than truth." He had little faith in aught that might be done by the valley-folk, either of wrong or right. "Be it how it may, it can be told at dawn." He went to sleep also. He did not know that Rita had heard. She had said nothing, as her way was.

Stele waked again while the light was yet dim. He rose without pause of thought, and roused Elsya, who could have slept more. Elsya waked with a fear in her mind's depth, but with another mood at its door. She said nothing till Stele asked, "Was it fact or dream that you told, when you roused us thus in the night?"

Elsya said, "You can learn that for yourself. You can seek as I."

"You can speak or not," said Stele, "as you will. You are for Thelmo to whip now, as I hope he will. If you spoke a true word, he may go to his death the while you sulk as you do. He may be dead before this."

Elsya answered quickly to that. "He was not dead in the night. They watched by an empty net. So I saw with my own eyes."

Stele said, "This is nothing at all, or it is a great thing. You may have done much. Will you tell us now? How learnt you all that you did?"

Rita looked at Elsya, saying nothing at all.

Elsya answered, more to her than to Stele, "I went on quiet feet. I stood at windows and doors. When I learnt enough to fear more, I went into the caves' mouth. I saw those who watched. I crept in, even to the god's pool. I heard their words. They have changed the way through the caves, so that those who come will fall down a steep place, even as they see the light at the end, and think that they have come through. They watch day and night, there being ever six that sit over the god's pool that they may see whom the trap takes, and the end to which they will fall."

"I know where they could do that," Stele said. "I think it is as you say. Well, we must have food. This is to be thought."

CHAPTER XXXIX.

ELSYA said, "We must find a way. He shall not come to that death in the dark!"

She spoke of Thelmo, thinking only of him, and, indeed, he was the most likely to come with speed, that she should be again in his arms, for she was of the kind which have maddened men since the world's dawn.

And then, Stele being silent, she spoke again, "If there be no better way, we must slay their guard in the night. You are a better fighter than they. I could kill one, and, it may be, more. Rita can throw well."

But Stele was still slow to speak, not because he could think of naught, but because he could see that of which he dreaded to think. For he saw that warning should be tried, and there was but one way. There were the unclimbable hills, which he knew that he could not scale; there was the lake, in which no man could fight the beasts and live, even could he swim so far, of which he had some doubt; and there was the way through the caves, which might be a poor chance, but was yet a chance that he ought to try.

He said, "Can you think of nothing better than that? We must find a way. But we cannot kill the whole guard. Not before help would be there. It is silly to say that. If you have nothing better to say, you should sit with a shut mouth."

He spoke as he did because he was in an evil mood, and while he spoke Elsya looked at him with a bloodless face, for she had seen what she should do, and it was that which she did not dare. She knew that they could not climb the unscalable hills, and it would be no use to Thelmo that one should be lost in the dark caves, as they had been told was the sure end of any who should go by that way; but there was a chance that one might swim the lake while the beasts were fed at the dawn, and she was Thelmo's wife, and she could swim three yards to Stele's two, and it was a thing that she ought to try, and she knew that she would not dare. She shook with fear at the thought.

And while they talked thus, Rita, who had eaten well, but had said nothing at all, reached for more of the nuts she loved, and ate with a steady will, which Elsya was vexed to see, for what was it to her, or to Stele either, that Thelmo should die thus? They had each other, which was enough. But it was her part to swim in the lake, which she would never dare. And so Thelmo would die, and she thought that she would die too.

Rita reached for the nuts again. She looked at Elsya, and she may have read her mind. She looked at Stele, and she knew his very well. She said, "When I have eaten all that I can I will go over the hills."

Stele looked at her, and there was fear in his eyes. "You cannot do that. I would not let you go. There is only one thing to be done: I will find my way through the caves."

Elsya knew what she ought to say then, but she was silent, being afraid.

Rita answered quietly, but with no change in her will, "You would be lost in the caves. There is only one way, and there is only one who can go."

She had a strange gladness in her heart, though Thelmo was nothing to her, and she guessed that he would have brought her to a quick death for his sister's gain. But she knew that she should not have come down from her own trees. She had been useless here, sitting apart, and her love of Stele did not blind her to the folly of the way she took, being one who was better to see than to do. But there was something here that they could not do, at which she did not think she should fail—something by which she felt that she might escape from the uncleanness of the life to which she had come down.

Stele said, "You shall not go. Even if you did, I should still go by the caves, so what use were there in that? I would rather think that you are safe here, and that we shall lie warm again when I shall come back."

Rita looked at him at that, and there was love in her eyes. "You would only die in the caves, which were loss to all. I also would lie warm when we meet. You must let me do this, which I think I can."

Elsya thought to herself, "She seems sure that she can, and, if so, it is the right way." She cared little for any so that Thelmo were warned, being of those who can love one at a time, rather than more. She said aloud, "You would take food?"

Rita said, "I shall not take more than I eat. It is not our way. I shall not die in that time."

Stele went to the door. He looked up at the eastern heights, over which the dawn came. They rose, cliff beyond cliff, very steep and grim, and the highest were slippery with ice and cloaked with snow. They were unclimbable hills.

He spoke with a firmer voice. "You cannot go by that way."

Rita came to his side. "But it is a thing I can do. Were it to be done with a club, I would stand aside. But I have good feet. I am not of those who can fall." And Stele saw, by the look in her eyes, that he might say what he would, but she would go her way.

He said, "I had not thought you to be one to do, while I should stay still."

Rita knew what he meant, and that it held all that was between them two. She said, "I am not one to toil, making things that I do not need, or bearing from place to place things that might lie as they are, but this is of a different kind. I will go now while the light is long."

She looked at Stele, as he at her, for they were not sure that they would come together again, and, as they did this, there came to them the memory of a lost thing, so that their eyes changed to a strange surprise, and then Rita knew that her mind searched for a thought that it could not keep, and it was all as before. But they parted, after that, with a holding kiss and a feeling that all was well.

Rita had gone for a time when Stele said, "I am going to try the caves. She will be glad to be met on that side if she comes through."

He went to the door again and looked up at the hills. The day was high, and the sun showed over the tops. There was a snowy height flanking the dawn to the north, which was of a clear rose. He wished he were with Rita in the clean hills, but he knew that those were heights that he could not climb.

Elsya said sharply, "Do not go. I shall be frightened alone. You will be lost in the caves."

He said, "It is a double chance. Do you want Thelmo to die?" At which she was still.

He was ashamed that he had not said that he would go at the first. Perhaps Rita would have stayed where she was if he had spoken a quick word. They were cold and terrible hills.

He came back into the hut. He packed all the food that he found. He said nothing more to Elsya, nor she to him. She sat with a white face, seeing snouts that rose in the lake. The water was red with blood, and her pearls were spilled, and she knew that it was a thing that she would not dare; but the fact stood that it was one that she ought to do, and her life was spoiled from this day, for either

Thelmo would die, or she would be ashamed to look in his eyes, for he would know that she had sat still.

So Stele went; and she sat until she was aware that the hut was watched, and she thought that there would be questions asked as to where Stele and Rita were, and she was afraid, being alone. She had never felt alone in her life as she felt then.

She went out at last, being afraid to sit longer alone, having the thoughts she had, and began to walk toward the entrance to the black caves, as though she would come closer to that from which her fear sprang. But I she was stopped on the way by a man that she did not know, who asked in a rude way what she would do.

She answered to that, boldly enough, "I walk as I will. What is that to you?" But he said, "You must walk in another way." He was curt of speech, as one who knew that the Prince her husband was no more than a dead man, and a new time come, so that she felt more alone than before.

She went back to the hut, feeling that she was watched now, and by those who looked also for Stele and Rita, being puzzled that they were not seen. She thought, "They will begin to ask me soon, and what shall I say? Shall I betray my friends if they threaten pain, being the coward that I am? Where can I go to be safe?"

She went out again, being followed, at which, on a sudden thought, she went to a place where she was sure that they would not come, being the stallion's field. She slipped through the fence, whereat he lifted his head, and then grazed as before. She went down the field, and sat, looking at the lake.

After a time the stallion can over to where she was. He stood a little way off, stretching his head down toward her, at which she got up and went to him, stroking his face with her hand. After that he stayed near her, and she felt less alone; but she could not keep her thoughts from those who had taken the danger that should have been hers.

Later in the day she went back and sat in the hut, eating some food; but she felt that she could not be alone there for the quiet hours, and she went out again in the dusk and sat where she had been before.

It was a warm night, and she sat there till the dawn, sleeping much of the time, with her head on her drawn-up knees, and having a dream at one time that Thelmo took the pearls from her neck to give to a braver girl, so that when she slept again she held them with a tight hand.

In the grey of the dawn she waked, shivering in a cold wind that came from the lake. The water was very still, and she thought,

"Shall I go now?" For the beasts would all be at the eastern end, waiting to be fed. But then she thought of their teeth, and she remembered that the lake was three miles long. "Do I know that they all go to be fed at that place? There may be those at the far end that have other ways." So she sat still.

But after that she thought, "I shall go in the end, and every minute that I sit here I lose many yards. I may lose my life while I sit here." So, at that, she got over the fence, not because she was of a good heart, but for fear that she should lose her life if she should be slower than that.

CHAPTER XL.

RITA went without haste or fear, choosing a quiet path, that she might not be stayed by those with whom she had no will to talk. She was not afraid of the hills, though she had a doubt of how cold they would be, for she had never met with a great cold, though there had been frost in the winter nights, and at times a little snow that fell through the trees, for her people would be warm in the cold days in the shelters that they built, and eating of the nuts that they had stored for that time.

But she knew that she could climb well, and she thought to make better speed in the steep heights than on level ground, for it was there that she could use her arms.

She climbed up the valley-wall at the eastern side, which was not easy to do, being seen by none (as she thought), and came to a place of cliffs, slippery and smooth and steep, where she made such way as could not have been done by one who had not lived in the trees, for she had feet that could hold with a sure grip, and she could judge her leap to an inch, grasping just as she would, either with feet or hands, and having no fear of a great depth. How she went up ever from height to height had been wonder to see for a man of our own day. Yet the hours passed, and though she was glad of the strong light of the sun, and of a clear air which was good to breathe, yet she was aware of a cold that she had not known in her life-days, and she had come to a field of ice, which was rough in some places, but not all. The smooth places were hard to climb, though she had feet which were not quick to slip.

The ice-field did not rise, but fell somewhat, not sloping toward the valley from which she came, but another way, to the south, so that there was a glad moment in which she felt that she could go down by that way; but when she thought of the way under the hills she knew that she was already more to the south, and that it was a poor chance that she could find a quick way if she went down by this southward gorge. She looked up at the sun and round at the hills, which she had watched as she came, and she knew that she must face the height which was at the far side of the ice.

When she had come to that height she saw no sure way either down or up, but many hollows and heights, and all rocky and very bleak. There was a cold wind at her back, which she would be glad to leave, going down if she could; yet she would not go by the wrong way.

It was at this time that she saw some large-horned deer that ran on a bare height, going the way that it seemed most like that she should, at which she thought (though she may have been wrong in that), "It must be in the lower vales that they find water and food. If I follow them they may show the best way down from the heights, for they must know the hills from their birth."

So she went on to keep them in sight with all the speed that she could, though she was tired now, as she had not known such feeling to be, and they led her well, as she thought.

At the last she looked down on a round valley that was a green depth in the hills. It went down very far, and in its midst a lake shone.

It was wooded at the one side, and would have been a fair place to seek had she been free of her life. But there was no way out. It was not her way. She had been wrongly led. She must turn to climb again, when she had thought that she was far down.

She knew then that it was that which she had not the strength to do, nor would the light hold, it being then near the dusk. All the day she had gone on, taking neither rest nor food. She saw trees by the lake, and she thought that she might find food of her own kind. She went down to the valley's depth, though she knew that she must climb again when the dawn came.

CHAPTER XLI.

ELSYA waded in for a few yards in a frightened way, the water being shallow in a receded place, and she looked right and left for a sign of the beasts she feared. Had a reed stirred or a ripple moved she might have run back, and have stayed where she was, but it was all vacant and still, and so she slipped into the deeper lake and swam out at the greatest pace that she could.

She thought little of the lake's length, for she had learnt to stay all day in the sea, if it were not too cold, but she did not go long at that speed, for her thoughts would change with her fears, which were very great.

At one time she would think that she should swim quietly and low, that she might not be observed, and at another that the sooner she could come to land the less must the danger be, so that she should use all the strength she had. At another she would think that she should save her strength for a great need. Then she swam very quietly, as she knew how, scarcely moving her limbs, and sometimes keeping under the water for a time. But then she would think that she would be safer if she could watch the surface of the lake, and must raise herself with a hard stroke, so that she could see far.

All this time she kept to the centre of the lake, where the stream ran, that she might have its help. The lake was no more than a wide gorge, the hills being sheer cliffs on either side that none could hope to climb. There was no way but to go on to the end.

And so she did, seeing the southern shore, low and green, and it was when she felt that she was safe at last, and was swimming faster than before, and in a good current—for she was coming to where the stream drained from the lake—that she saw the snout of one of the dreaded beasts that seemed adrift on the lake.

He must have seen her as she saw him, for the snout came round, so that he was almost across her way, and then he came very fast, swimming with feet and tail, his head half out of the lake, and the water breaking round his jaw. Then his head went down and he made a snap at her arm.

She gave a swift twist to one side, so that the jaws closed to no more than the water gave, but it was so close that she felt the beast's snout as it brushed her neck, and she had a panic thought that it had broken her pearls and that they would be lost in the flood, and at that fear she turned, as a woman will if her child be seized in a dog's teeth, and gave battle as best she could.

It would have been the beast's way to have caught her by arm or leg, and to have pulled her down till her breath should fail, and he could make his meal of a drowned thing. She did not know this, nor did he know how long she could hold her breath if she would, but, having avoided his jaws, she dived in a way which he did not expect, coming up beneath, so that she grasped his neck, and their bellies met, they being of a like size. He was not holding her, but she held him, and in a way that he did not choose, so that he had no use for his jaws; and as he struggled and splashed he was aware of two pains, and his sight went, for her fingers had found his eyes. And after that she let him go free.

CHAPTER XLII.

STELE was not one to move with a rash speed into a danger that he had not measured with care. When he went out, he took not only his axe and such food as he could, he carried also a spear of a length to guide his steps in the dark. Not that he meant to move without the light of a torch, which would have been to bring a poor chance to none. But he would have trouble enough to make his way to the cave-mouth without hindrance or note, being armed as he was. Should he be stopped with a torch in hand, it would tell where he would go louder than any word could deny. But for that he would have taken a torch to be lit at one of those in the god's cave. He thought it better than that to take one of those torches from its grip in the wall. Yet either to take or light might not be easy to do, for Elsya had told that there were those who watched in that cave, and he must pass them by force, or unseen.

As to force, he had called in vain when Elsya had spoken first, and so he thought still of her plan, for they would have had to overcome all the strength of the valley-folk before they could undo the trap they had made, even though the guard were down before aid should reach. Yet he thought now of a sudden rush and some good axe-blows, which would take him through. He thought little of the valour of these men, or of their skill in strife. But there was the torch, which might not be easy to take in a quick way, and there was the fact that Elsya was left, and there might be doubt as to how she would fare if it were known that he had passed the cave, having slain men to win way. He did not think overmuch of that, for women must take their own chances at such times, but he saw that she was in peril enough. He would go unseen, if he could.

That might not be easy to do, yet he had a hope, thinking that the men would watch and listen for those who might come from the depths of the caves, rather than by the outer way. He was one who could move without sound, though he was large.

147

He gained so much as to enter the caves unseen, and he came to where the watch, which was of six men, was grouped on the edge of the god's pool. They looked and pointed at something which was below, but what it was he could not see, being farther back, nor had he care to know. He saw only that he could pass unseen at their backs, but for the torch, which he must have, and they might look round if he made noise in that, or it were slow to come loose.

He passed but six feet behind their backs as they bent, and as he did this he had a good thought. With the blunt end of the spear he gave a push to one of the bending men. It was just a quick jab, given between the buttocks of one who bent far to look, but it was enough to send him over the edge. As he fell he screamed, clutching at the man on his left, who was dragged over alike. They fell with a great splash. Stele could hear a rush and turmoil in the pool below. He guessed that they had been watching the god, and that he had given him a good meal. The other men did not think to look round. They thought only that he who fell had leaned over too far. Their eyes were better fixed on the pool than before.

Though Stele listened he did not pause. He was quick to take a torch from the wall, finding it to come away without effort or noise, and was quick also to take the inward turn of the rock, where its light could not be seen by those who watched, should they look round. He would not go farther than that till he had seen what was the snare that had been laid for those who might be next to come through the hills.

This was easy to see by the light he had, he being so warned, yet it must have been no less than a swift death for those who would have come without thought. For at this place the floor of the cave by which they would come was wide, and there were loose boulders that lay about on which men would be bruised who walked not in the right way. And among these was one very large, which was the mark of the path, which passed by its side.

This boulder had been moved, as had other smaller ones which would be earlier reached, so that those who would come, having no great light, and moving with no more care than do those who come by a known way, would be off the path without heed, till those who were first would be aware that it sloped downward more than it should, and, at the same time, that their feet slipped, for the path had been made smooth with fat. This might have been less sure than it was, for those in the rear, being all joined, might have pulled them back, but that their own feet would have little grip, for the level floor also had been made greasy and smooth, though less so than the slope, that it should not be noticed too soon. It was a good trap, for the slope would have shot them all down to the depth of the god's pool, where they could not have done much, after such a fall, and being held in one string. So the god would feed, and if any should struggle free, more or less, that was for the dealing of those who watched.

Stele saw that it was a good plot, but he had little time to admire. He must go on while his light would last. All his mind must be bent to recall, to recount, to measure, to watch lest he overlook either turning or gap in the dark walls.

He went on for some hours, now in doubt, and now sure that he was in the right way; after which there was a long time that he thought he was lost, and was of half a mind to turn back; and then he came to a gap that must be jumped, and that he knew. There was no doubt of that. He must have come half the way, and be right still. He thought that the King might have willed it to be thought it was that worse than it was. He was in better heart for that, but did not lessen his care.

He was the more vexed when he came again to the gap he knew, but at that side that showed he had turned round, and, had he crossed it again, he had been on his way back.

He must turn again, and go with a greater care. It was hard to guess what he had done. He went on at a slow pace, thinking hard. He chose a way more to the right, even though he thought it wrong. He was soon back from that. It led nowhere at all.

He went on, trying another turn. It went far, coming at last to a place of shallow pools. That was new, and he turned back again, after drinking, which he was glad to do, though the water had an ill taste.

He was scarcely lost, for he got back again to the place he knew, but he could not find the way forward from that.

He tried again, and found a way that might be wrong or right; he went in doubt for some hours, and as he went the doubt grew, but so also did the length of the way back, which he was the less ready to try. He saw that if he turned back, being on the right way, his case was evil indeed.

When he became sure that he had gone wrong he turned back, but not long after that he came to a turn of which he felt better hope. He went down this but a short way, when he came to a sudden fall, and slipping there on a loose stone he came down, with a twisted foot, and his torch went out as he fell.

The torch could be kindled anew, if he would work for sufficient time with the means he had, and, being hot, it was a thing to be started in haste, for it would be harder when it became cool. So he

149

sat where he was, twisting it in the hollow socket which he had brought for that need, and after a time it broke again into flame.

He was glad of this, but slow to move, for his ankle was swollen and hot; also, he knew by that fall that he was again in a wrong way.

Yet when he found how slowly he must now move, and with what pain, he resolved to go on, for, though it were a poor chance, it was better than none, and to go back was beyond hope—with the strength he had left—that he would come through.

He went on then for what seemed a very long time, though he could but crawl, and rested, and went on again. He went on till his food was gone, having stayed for sleep at one time, and at the last he came to a rocky wall, and knew that it had been all for naught, and it would be a strange chance indeed that would make him more than a dead man. He had little hope, yet he must search round with the torch which was now but a short length, as a trapped rat searches the bars; and, doing so, he came to the low horizontal slit in the rock which had been shown to him once before, only now he was on the wrong side. He knew that it was the same, for, when he thrust in the torch as far as he might, he could see the bones that he had been shown before, only where he had seen a skull and an outstretched arm he saw now the bones of a leg that was stretched out and of another that was drawn up, as they had been at the last when the man died.

Stele knew that he had come to an ill end. There was nothing surer than that. He let the torch lie so that it flickered and went out. With enough toil it might be kindled again, but it was nearly done, and he did not think that it would be of a longer use. If there were anything to be done now it must be done in the dark. If he were once through that narrow slit he could find his way to the light, even with his leg as it was, but he had little hope of that.

He lay for a time without movement, thinking what might be done. Could he cut through with his axe? He judged the thickness of the rock to be the length of three men, lying heel to head. He would need to cut a large way. He was bigger than most. He tried to push his head in at the place where he lay. It went in, and then stuck so that he had some pain in his neck when he had pulled it forth. He had had a moment of panic fear when he had thought that it would not come, so that his heart beat very fast for a time, as he had never known it to do.

He would not be in a haste to try that again. Yet he might not have tried at the best spot. He crawled along from end to end—about three tens of feet—feeling the height of the slit with his hand, and with his spear, as far as it would go. Being still in doubt, he did this three times before he chose what he thought to be the best place. He did not wish to waste strength through not choosing with care.

Then he began to chip with the axe. The rock did not powder, but flaked, giving him a little hope at the first, though not much, being very hard; and when he had worked till he was tired, he rested a while, and made a count, by which it seemed that he would get through at that rate in three moons, or in two at the best. It was little more than a guess. He could not tell to a ten of days, but what did it matter if it were two moons or three? His strength would not last, nor his axe, to a tenth of either. Counting thus, he might have ceased an effort that was so vain; yet this he did not do, for he was one to take the last ounce from the scales of chance. He thought, "If help come, they may hew from that side, and will be the sooner through. Also, the noise of the axe may be heard, if any pass, and that will bring help. They could give water and food, pushing them with a long spear, and I could live as long as I need." He thought also that he could give warning to any who should be about to try the passage, and so do that for which he had come.

So he worked till he was wearied again (which was in a shorter time than before); and then his mind turned to wonder whether Rita were over the hills. If she were so, it might mean that the passage would soon be tried in the King's wrath, which was a new hope. He chipped again, though for a shorter time than the last, and rested again. He wished that Rita were there. If he perished thus, how soon would she learn his death? She would say little, as her way was. Would she go back to the trees?

CHAPTER XLIII.

RITA came down from the hills. She saw a wide plain, with squared fields having one colour of growth, showing that the plants they held had become the slaves of mankind; she saw also many dwellings of men.

It was a greater land than she had been able to see from the cave-mouth. She was of a good courage, though not one to aggress without cause. While she had lived in the trees, she had not doubted that she was sufficient for her own safety. Even the tree-leopards turned aside if they met one of her people. They did not like the nuts that could be thrown so straight and hard, nor the speed with which the tree-folk gathered at the call of one of their kind. They knew that they would not move in peace through the high boughs should they wake a feud which would be taken up by all. Only if a child were alone in a leafy place.

But since she had come down from the trees she had known fear. She was in a hateful place, a place always of danger and of frequent dirt. She had chosen this for a love which she did not regret, but she saw it with clear eyes.

She looked on this strange land, where men were busy to do, and had (as she thought) no leisure left to live, and she was reluctant to go down to take the chance of being in the power of such, even for the warning which she had come to give.

She did not think to fail, but she knew that there was no haste while she could watch the steps to the cave, as she did, for none could enter unseen; and as she looked she thought of another way. Why should she not wait in the cave? None would come there but those whom she knew, and who would know her, and for whom her warning was meant. Could she enter the caves unstayed?

She could not see that there was any guard at the cave-mouth, or that there were those who walked by that way. She thought that it might be left alone, except when the King was within and they waited for his return. She looked far over the plain, and she thought she saw a gathering or tumult of many men. It seemed that there were few or none in the nearer ways, or who toiled in the nearer fields, as men must who have made slave of a growing plant, and are slaves also to it, by the law which none may break or avoid. It seemed that there must be that which drew all to the farther side of the land, both the women and men, but though she stood high and her sight was clear for many miles in a pure air she could not tell what it was.

Well, she would wait in the cave-mouth, and give warning to those who came, which would be Thelmo by the best guess, Elsya being where she was.

So she made her way down the last slope, and came to a flattened track, such as she had not seen before, for it was paved with flat stones. Stele would have looked at it with judging eyes, counting the men that must have toiled for the making of so great a thing, and wondering how the stones were smoothed; but Rita thought it a foolish toil for a poor end. She did not give it two thoughts, but she was glad that it was empty of men, and she made her way with speed till she came to the crescent of steps, and mounted them, meeting no one at all, and so entered to the cave-mouth.

She had thought to go inward to the furnished caves which were at the end of the first passage, where they had spent the night-hours when first they had come through.

But when she came to the face of the dark she had little will to walk in a blind way. The hole under the hills was a fearful thing to one who was born on the twisted boughs of a high tree. The grey, cold walls and the closing roof were like a weight that would bear her down. The dark of night beneath the cloudiest sky in the forest-land, where no smoke rose, was a clear light to the blackness of that hateful hole. Every instinct, in a body alive to feeling, as that of one who is bred in streets can never be, warned her against the entering of such a cave. It was true that she had been there before, but that was with Stele, and for him, when love had conquered fear, or her will had held it below.

Now she would do no more than sit in the narrow cleft that approached the roofed cave, where she could still see the sun's light, and something of the sky and of the plain afar. She thought it could not be long before Thelmo would come.

But she sat there for some hours, and none came. At times she heard a sound as of a steady tapping within the dark hollow of the cave. She might have thought more of that had she meant to venture therein. As it was, being tired, she thought more of sleep. She did not wish to be caught in sleep by whoever might come first to the cave-mouth, who might be no more than the servants of Thelmo, preparing for him to come, and who might not know her at all. She did not know how they would deal with such as she, but she guessed that she might wake, at the best, with shackled limbs, or it might be with a knife in her neck, being good meat, as she was.

Yet, being weary from her coming over the hills, she went from time to time to the platform from which she could gain a wider view, and seeing none coming from there she went back and had a short sleep, being able to wake when she would.

It was at the third of such times of sleep that she waked from a dream which had vexed her rest. It did not seem to have been a good dream, though it had been about Stele. It had been of the dark caves, and of that narrow slit in the rock which had been a terror to see, thinking of what it must have been to him who had tried to crawl through and had been stuck in the midst.

But she could not tell what the dream was. It was one which her mind would chase, seeming to come very near, but it could not catch. When she tried to think of the dream, she thought always of the bones that the torch had shown, and she could not clear them out of her mind, though she knew that the dream had not been of them.

While she tried to recall this dream, the tapping within the cave was commenced again, and the two seemed one in a way which she could not understand. She thought for the first time: what could it be? Having heeded it once, it would not go from her mind. It went on but for a short time, and when it ceased, she listened long for it to commence again. It had become to her as that which could open the dream and give ease to her mind.

She was not one who would hurry thought, or cast it aside, as men must do who have toils to take at an ordered hour. She listened for the sound to commence again, which it was not quick to do. When it did, she went somewhat into the dark of the cave that she might better hear what it was. She was afraid to do this, but was of too high a courage to let fear rule when there was a wish in her mind.

When she heard it thus (for the sound was louder and of a different tone when she stood under the cave's roof) she guessed at once what it was. At least, she guessed that it was made by one who was caught in the cave's trap, and with that thought there came a swift knowledge of whom it would be. "Stele hath come under the hills."

She went with quick steps to the cave's wall. She bent somewhat, feeling along it with her hand, as she moved inward, till she came to the place where the gap was. Here she stayed, but there was nothing to hear, for the tapping had ceased as she approached. "Stele," she called through the slit.

CHAPTER XLIV.

STELE had worked as hard as his strength would let him do, and he was not weak, as we know. But it was not as it would have been could he have stood upright, giving the axe a good swing. Also, he was getting weaker from hour to hour through lack of water and food, which was why he must work for a shorter time, and rest longer between. His leg did not get better from the rest it had, but was more swollen, and of a sharper pain should it be dragged as he worked.

Worse than these was the fact of which he had not thought until the trouble came, that every foot which he should cut into the rock would make the work harder to reach in such a way that he could smite well, unless he should cut a much wider gap than he had counted to do.

As he worked thus he saw that he would never cut his way through with his living hands, and he went on less from any hope of that than that the noise might be heard, and because he was of a stubborn kind.

When Rita called as she did, he had ceased to smite with a weak hand, or to think how his leg throbbed, but lay with a wandering mind, not being troubled or aware of the gin in which he was caught. But her voice waked him to his own life. It waked him less to fear of the pain and peril in which he lay than to anger that he was fallen thus, who had never been used to call for help, nor had he thought of Rita but as one who would live in the safety of his own arm.

Yet he was very glad of her voice, both for the love they had, and because it brought hope of life. He thought also that it showed she had come safely over the hills. His first word was of that.

"Yes. It is I. I am here, having lost myself like a fool. Did you come safely through? Are you unhurt by the cold and the bitter heights?"

156

"I am well. I found food and rest in a high vale. It is good that you are here too." She did not doubt at the first that all would be well, they being so nearly met.

But as they talked more, and she learnt how he lay, and how he was nearly spent, and how little he had cut through, she saw that there was but one way, which must be taken with speed, and from which she did not shrink now, though she would not face it before.

She said, "I will find Thelmo or the King."

Stele said, "The King is a vain hope. He will laugh that I lie thus."

"He will not laugh when he hears why we came."

"He may not, or he may. He may not believe. Tekla is the better chance."

Rita would have put her last, if at all. But she could not say he was wrong.

"I will seek her first, if you will. There shall be water and food brought."

She did not lose time in more words.

CHAPTER XLV.

RITA went on for some time through the strange land, being stayed by none, and seeing none but some children that were less than half grown, though able to run by themselves, and an old man that lay in the sun, with a weeding-tool in his hand. She did not blame him for that. She might have thought him sane in a mad land. She roused him with a foot at his ribs in a gentle way, for she must have speech with some one. She might wander long without finding those she sought, losing much time, if no worse evil should breed. She said, "Can you tell me where I can find the King? Where I can find the King's daughter or his son?"

The man did not understand her words very well. He was dazed with sleep. He had never seen a tree-woman before, though he knew that there were such in the great woods in other parts of the world. Once, in his youth, he had eaten part of a man of the trees, who had been caught on the ground, when he had been in another place. That was before this land was as great or as safe as it was now. As to it being safe, it was fighting for its life on that day against the swamp-rats' teeth, but he was too old to be called to fight, so he was not greatly troubled by that. He could lie in the sun.

When he understood what Rita would know, he pointed in the right way, though he was not sure that he waked.

"The King's house is on that road. The King's daughter, or his son, will be farther to find. They will be at the war. But the King will sit in his house."

There was no more to be learnt from him. Rita went on.

She made her way with more ease than she might have done at another time, and when the sun was very low in the sky she came to the King's house, and stood where she would be seen.

It was a house of more state than he could have when he went to the valley-folk, as she had seen him first, but the five sat in a row before him, as they had done then, seeming to see naught, but having their hands near to the knives they wore.

Rita thought, "It is the second from the right who will throw, if the King wills. Could I be quicker than she?"

She saw all, but she gave no more sign than they.

The King knew her at once. He had troubles enough, and his mind was on greater things, but he had thought for all. He was not pleased that she had come there. He was quicker than she to speak.

"How left you the vale?"

"I came over the hills. There is that which you should know. Stele came also, through the caves, but he lies at the wrong side of the wall, needing swift aid lest he die."

This was a foolish speech, as she had leisure to think at a later hour, but not now. She should have said what it was that she had come to tell before talking of Stele at all. But she was not used to dealing with such as the King was, and she had half her thought on the one who was second from the right, who she felt sure was alert to throw.

The King took no heed of her middle words. He heard the first and the end. He thought that they had defied him in a vain attempt to escape. He laughed a little at that.

He said, "Had he found his way through, you had not been here. He is well caught. There is none can come through the hills and live. Let him stay where he is, or go back, if he think he can."

He thought, "She might tell that which should not be known here. She should have a quick death."

Rita made a quick bend as the knife came, so that it passed the side of her neck. She knew well how to move with speed if the need were, and not to show before what she was thinking to do. It was unlucky for one that stood behind, and took that which was meant for her. But he is not in this tale.

The King was a just man. He saw that the knife had passed where her neck had been. The fault was not with the throw. He saw that Rita was gone. She had had enough of those knives. She did not think to dodge four others at once.

The King was not fevered in mind. He said aloud, so that all might hear, "The tree-woman is not to save or to keep. She is meat to catch." He did not think that she would live long, she being what she was, and his people that which they were, nor that she would hold speech, either for gain or loss. He turned his regard to the more urgent and greater things.

Rita ran well. She was glad that the dark was not far. She dodged stones, and was near to death from a well-flung spear. She came to a wooden hut in which goats were tied. As she ran by it, she caught up a stone which would fill her hand. She sprang to the roof

159

of the shed. She threw as hard as she might. A man fell with a broken skull. There was meat, if they would.

She outpaced a pursuit that had become more cautious than it had first been. She shook it off. She hid till the night fell.

When it was dark she went back to Stele, but it was a poor tale that she had to tell.

CHAPTER XLVI.

WHEN she had told her tale, Stele was silent for some time. He was weak of body, and his mind wandered at times, though it would become very clear after that. He did not blame her at all, seeing that, in her own way, she had done bravely and well, though he thought that she might have brought it to a better end had she been wiser of word. But even that was not sure.

Anyway, that was done.

He thought of many ways, for he was slow to believe that he was to die there, but there was none that was any good. He said at last, "There is no more to be done. I must die here. You must go back to the trees where you can live in peace and forget that you had come down."

She said, "I shall not do that, as you should know, if you know me at all. Nor do I see why you should die. I can fetch water and food when the light comes, and you can live well enough, if I push it through, as I shall. Soon or late, Thelmo or Tekla will come, and will listen to what I say, which will change all."

"That is what you would to be," Stele answered, "but is unlikely from end to end. You cannot get water and food in a land where you are hunted by all. At the best they will chase you here, and if they do not follow you in, they will close the hole, or catch you if you go forth again. You will lose your own life and do no better than give me a slower death.

"As to Thelmo and Tekla, in whom you trust, they may not come for many days, if at all. For you can see that they are at a great strife, of which we know naught except that it goes ill. For had it gone well they had been here before this. Besides, you have seen that there are few, either of women or men, who are left in the land. I think they fight at a great loss. Those of whom we talk may be now dead, or if they live now they may be dead sooner than I.

"You must go to the hills, where you may still live. You may find a way to our own land, where you can be as you were."

"I shall not do that. I shall wait here, as I said."

Stele was angered at that, though he was glad too. He said, "You are my wife, and should do as I say, even though I am near to death. It is vain to sit there. I am more near to death than you know. My leg is of a great heat, but except for that it is like a dead thing."

Rita did not answer at once. It had come into her mind that her arms were long and of a great strength. Why should not she use the axe? She felt along the gap in the rock. She was smaller than Stele. Was there not a place where she could squeeze through?

She felt it for all its length, and backward again. She found what she thought to be the best place, at least for the start. She could not feel beyond that. But she could push her head and shoulders in at that place when she lay flat. She said, "I shall try to come through."

"It is vain. No one could. I saw that on the day when it was shown by the torch's light. You will stick fast and die."

It was a fearful thought, not being a death that would be chosen by most, and least of all by one who had no love for a close space. Her heart paused in its fear. She said, "Well, I shall try."

"If you try, let it be where I have cut for some way. It is shorter risk."

He showed her where it was by his voice. It was at the place which she had chosen at her own side. There was hope in that.

As she began to crawl under the rock lying very flat, and wriggling forward with outstretched arms, she had a doubt that she could keep straight, having no light. She saw that if she would do this she must try to force her way through, even though it should get tighter at every inch. If she should move to left or right, as it might be the easier to breathe and wriggle on, she might soon be so lost that she would not know where she would be. She might come out at last on the side at which she went in. Or she might be nearly through, and wriggle back to be fixed at last where she could move no more. It might be that that was how he had died in the dark whose bones were so near her now. But she was not as he. She had Stele's voice for her guide.

Stele had chipped away so much of the rock that he could wriggle under to half his length without feeling the roof. Beyond that his head could not go, but his arm could, and this he put in to its length, feeling for which might be the better way, and hoping to reach her hand.

Inch by inch Rita came on. Now her head was held. Should she push if forward or try to draw back? She pushed it on, feeling the rock tighten, and then it was in a better place. She found that if her head could get through her body would follow, though it might be

162

with pain at times. If there were any space over her head, though it were but a shallow inch, she would keep it down so that it did not feel the roof, for, being thus, she might try to think that she was in a free place and not doomed to a dreadful death. There were times when the rock held her down, and she would cry out to Stele, as though he could give any help, but for the most part she saved her breath, moving slowly, as he urged her to do...and so there came a time when their hands met.

But though their hands met they were little helped, for she found at the next moment that she could not come through at that place, there being a spot where the roof sank more than at most, and they were still some distance apart, their two arms being stretched as they were. She must loose hands, trying to wriggle somewhat aside.

This she did well enough for a short way—it may have been two feet or three—and then she found that she had come again to a place where her head was held. She tried to move back at that, and found that there was pressure also upon her back. She seemed to be held down both before and behind. She tried to move to either side, and could find little help. If it were better at one spot it was worse at another. It must have been that the way by which she tried to with-draw was not quite that by which she had come.

When she felt herself to be so held, and could find no way of re-lief, there was a moment that her courage failed. She struggled with a foolish strength, as though she would lift the mountain that held her down. She did not know that she screamed. As the panic passed, and she knew that she had done but a vain thing; she had to learn that it was worse than that, for she had used her strength to force herself into a tighter place.

Now she lay so that her head could not move, nor her back, nor could she tell in which way to try for relief. She was in such fear for a time that she did not heed the voice of Stele who called to her, hearing the sobs she gave. She knew how fast her heart beat in its fear, and that she must use all her will that she should not waste her strength once again. She would have liked to strain with her back till her spine broke. She did not heed that her head bled much, being scraped of skin, though this had been so, more or less, from the first, or that her body was in a like case.

She would have given most of the life she had to be in the free space which to Stele was a trap of death. It seemed then that no man could have a real grief if he could move his head, and his limbs could go as they would.

"Stele," she said, "I am caught. It is here that my bones will be." She wrenched again at the word, but in a useless toil, not knowing which way to pull, and feeling held on all sides.

He called to her, "Do not haste. Lie as flat as you can. You must move to the left to be back in the place you were. If you make less haste you can feel for the better way."

She said, "You do not know how I am. I am held down that I cannot move. I cannot breathe as I would. I would die now if I might."

For the first time he thought of the spear. He should have done that before, but his own mind was becoming a blurred thing, with the toil he had gone through, and the hunger and thirst, and the pain of the wrenched leg. He groped for it now, and pushed the blunt end about till he felt where Rita was, and sounded the space that was between her and him, scraping the rock above and below, feeling for freer space. At the last he said, "It is this way, if at all, unless you do better to go back. Will it help if you hold the spear and I pull at the right time?

But she laughed at this, giving words in reply that had no meaning at all, for she knew not that which she said.

It was a mood that passed at a later hour, when she waked to life with a thought that she slept in the high boughs where her nest had been in her young days, and then screamed as she found that she could not move, but she had scarcely time for her fear to rise to its full height before Stele spoke in a quiet voice, and the spear haft was against her hand.

Her mind for that moment was on Stele more than herself, so that she became of a calmed will to be at his side if she yet might, as she had meant at the first. Holding the spear as he urged, and with his pulling at the right time, her shoulder moved for a short way, and it was less pressed than before. She was so that she could draw her head for an inch back and then sideways for more than that. She felt on that side with her hand. It was but a short way, and a better space.

Inch by inch she moved till she was much nearer to Stele. She thought at one time that she had but to rule her will, and to move with no haste, and she would come clear at the end. But it was not to be. She came at last to such a place that her head was not pressed. It could lift for a short space. But her back was so held that she could not move it at all. The roof pressed her spine at the root so that she was in great pain, but to try to move it either to right or left, either forward or back, was to make the pain worse; but beyond that it did nothing at all.

At this time she was so near to Stele that she had his hands in her own, and he was of a mind to use his strength that she should be wrenched free. But when he found that she screamed at the first pull, wrenching her hands back and loose from his own, he stopped (as he thought) for a time, till she should have fixed her mind to endure.

But she said, "You cannot do that, unless you would have me die at once. You would pull me out with a broken back, and with I know not what hurts beside, if my arms came not off before that. It is much that my arms are free, and that I can breathe as I will. But I would that I could have used the axe to get us both free, as I thought to do."

As she said this she saw that the hope of life was a past thing, both for him and her, and as the thought came there was another that moved in the dark of her mind, but so that she could not catch it at all, yet it made the death that was at their door a less dreadful thing than she would have thought it to be. She saw in a clear light that it was well that she had come down from the trees, though it was ending here as it did, and that it would have been a poor thing that she should have tried to live the life that Stele would have had her to do. He would not be vexed now when the women of his tribe should say that her arms were too long (of which she had had pride from her first years), or that she was useless for the toils with which they burdened their lives. She saw that death was not so dreadful a thing that one should step from its path at a great cost, but that it was much that they had done well while they yet lived, taking the risks they did, though it were for a warning that they would not give. She knew not then that her back was in a great pain, nor was her mind irked that she could not move as she would.

Stele spoke to her once or twice, calling (as it were) from the mist that was in his own mind, and when he found that she did not heed he had a fear that she was already dead. But his voice came to her when he called again, though it seemed that it was a far thing, and her hands closed on his in a firm grip which did not loose when they died.

CHAPTER XLVII.

THE King sat in his house, and before him, as ever, was the line of the sexless wives, but Thelmo and Tekla were not there.

It was high noon when Elsya came. She was weary and soiled of body, and she wore but a torn rag.

The King looked at her in wonder which would have found quick word, but that he was never hasty of speech, and when she saw that the seats of Thelmo and Tekla were bare she exclaimed in a sharp fear, "They have not gone by the caves? They must be stayed in haste!"

The King was in an angered doubt as to how she should have come there at all. He was not pleased to think that she had found a way. Yet he saw that her coming at that time was a god's boon. He was one who saw all in its true place, as one who looks from a height. He would know both how she had come, and why they should not go, but he was not of those who ask two things in one breath. He said only, "Why should they not go by the caves?"

"It is a sure death if they do. There is a plot among the valley-folk. They have changed the path in the dark. Those who go next by that way will fall to the god's pool."

"Have they so?" said the King. "Then they will be soon dead. They were ever a futile folk."

He thought of how he had been in their midst, with but half a score of his own, and they had not lifted a spear. Then he asked, "How did you come?"

Elsya was as quick as he, though she had a less cool mind. She saw that he was not troubled, nor roused to haste, and she knew that Thelmo was not gone to the caves. She answered what she was asked.

"I swam the lake while the beasts fed. I had need to kill one at the last. But for that I came clear." She told, at some length, how it had died. We need not pause for a known tale, but it was much to her. She thought she had done well. She was one who loved praise,

166

which the King gave, though his words were fewer than hers. But her tale went on after that. She had gone of need for a far way down the river-bank, seeking a firm path, and had come at last through the swamp, which was neither water nor land. The King was amazed at that, as he might well be. He said, "What of the rats?"

"I saw one that looked out from the reeds. It had a lame leg, by which I think I was saved. It showed teeth, but I stood, being in a place where I could not run. But I was in a great fear. It was the first I have seen. I had not thought them of that size. I think it was larger than I."

"It was less than that," said the King. "Saw you naught else?"

"I came on a woman's bones, and on this rag, which was caught on the near reeds. This I took, having swum the lake bare."

"You saw no rats but the one? Then it is worse than I thought. It has been well for you, for had you come on another day, you had died in that swamp. You had been torn prey for a hundred jaws. But the rats are gathered to take our land, and our people fight now at the long stockade. Thelmo and Tekla are there. It is a good chance that you have come as you did. You will hearten the host. But why did not your brother come?"

"Stele does not swim as do I. Yet he ventured first. He tried the way of the caves. Rita also came before me. She tried the way of the hills. I was afraid, so that I did not start till the dawn."

She told this truth for her brother's name, though it was hard to say. The King did not show his thoughts. If he had wonder or shame that those he had planned to slay should have taken such risk, it was a thought that did not rise to the light. He said only, "You did well to fear, taking such risk as you did." He had no doubt that Stele and Rita were dead, or on a short way to that end. It did not cross his thought to send rescue or aid. As to that, we may say that he had cares enough, as we learn what he then knew. He thought, as he had done before, that Thelmo had a wife of a good kind.

As he spoke, a woman came with word from the host. He had a message thus every time that the shadow moved to a marked point.

"How does it go?" said the King. He spoke first, for the woman was short of breath, having run well. "It goes hard."

"Is that Thelmo's word?"

"The Prince said, 'Tell the King that the rats are many, but the line holds.'"

"How goes it with those of the Left Wing?"

"They ride out yet, when the press is most hard on the stockade, charging from gate to gate, but they have lost much."

"How many are left?"

"There may be four score at the most."

"The Princess is unhurt?"

"The Princess Tekla still leads."

"It is well," said the King. His face showed no sign, yet he knew, if there were but four score alive of the riders of the Left Wing, which were the best strength that he had, that his land and all those that he ruled might be at their last day. He had thought of this for many hours as he sat still, pondering how many and who might be led through the caves to the safety of the hidden vale, should the fight be lost. Yet of this he had said nothing, even to those of his own house, for it is not well, when men fight, that they be aware of a backward way.

He said to Elsya, "You have done well, and a greater thing than you yet know. You shall neither loiter nor haste, but go to your own house, eating food there, and clothing yourself as your state is, and come again here to me."

So Elsya did this, and the sun was somewhat lower than its noon height when she came again to the King.

The King said, "The people were in a poor heart when it was known at the dawn that the swamp-rats came anew, being in a great host, and that they had crossed the width of the barren land. They said, 'Where is she whom the gods sent? They have had her back to themselves, that she should not die with our deaths.' If you go to Thelmo now, and be shown to those who still live, it may be they will hold the line. So I think it will be, and I will stake all on this throw."

Then he spoke to the five, and they rose without word or look, going to their deaths at the King's word, and leaving him where he was, without service or guard. He had thought, "They have six knives each, and each knife, as they throw, will be a rat's death. It is thirty sped. Who could say but that were the turn of the high tide? The meal is not cooled at one breath, be it first or last, yet each breath is a needed thing." He would save his land if he might.

Elsya went on foot, of which she was glad, for though she had no fear of a horse, she had no practice upon its back, and she had a dread lest she should do ill in the eyes of all.

She went with a guide before and with the King's guard at the rear. They would have drawn eyes, even though she had not been there, for they never moved but where the King was.

She came first to those who were withdrawn from the line, for none can fight without rest in the sun's heat, and the rats' attack had not ceased since the dawn rose. Thelmo had ruled that men should strive for a space in the front line, and rest for a double space after that, before they should fight again. That had been at the first. Later in the day he had made the times of fight and rest of an equal length. Then he had cause to lengthen his line, as the rats spread more to the north, and the women had been called to take their share of the strife. Now men must fight for two spaces in the line, and must rest but one, for only so was the line held.

Elsya came to those who sat on the ground. They bound wounds. They looked downward, with sombre eyes, as but waiting their time to die.

Yet, when they saw her come thus, they forgot that their knees were weak, leaping up with a glad shout. "It is the god's aid at the last. God's daughter comes to the war."

They cried her name out of sight to the south, and to the far north, above the sound of the men that fought, and the squealing of rats, which was a noise that did not lessen or change.

Elsya had a great pride at that cry, loving it better than most things that the world holds, unless it were the beads at her throat.

So she came to where Thelmo fought. His folk held the line of the long ditch which had been cut where the level rose from the plain. At its inner edge there was a low stockade of half the height of a man, so that those who stood there could smite over its top at the rats that climbed up the ditch's side, while their legs would be safe from the rats' teeth. Those who stood thus could look far over the plain, but they could not see where the army of the rats ceased, so that it seemed useless to slay.

Thelmo did not stand in one place. He moved ever behind the line, giving aid where the need was the most sore, for there were places where the ditch was so filled with the dead that it was easy to mount to the stockade's edge, and at such spots there was ever a sharp strife, the rats leaping clean over at times, and at the necks of women and men, who must throw them off as they could, and perhaps draw back from the line with a spurt of blood at the throat that they could not stay.

CHAPTER XLVIII.

THELMO turned at that shout, and saw where Elsya came, even as soon as she saw him. At the first sight, he was too glad to give thought to the wonder of how she came.

As to her, she looked only at him, seeing not the savage sea of the rats, over which those must look who stood at the front, till she gained the strength of his arms, and felt that she had come to a safe place, as he caught her up from the ground; for, as we know, she was much smaller than he.

Yet as they kissed, his thoughts went beyond their own joy to what she was to his land. "You must go higher yet," he said, at that thought; "you must let all men see.

He made his shield level as he spoke, on his left arm, and he lifted her with his right, so that she sat on the shield, drawing up her feet at the side. There was good space on the shield, which was large and round, she being as small as she was.

When she was well set, he lifted the shield high over his head, so that all might see, at which the shout broke out anew.

So raised, she saw much which was ill to view. She looked once at the rat-thronged plain, and she had looked more than enough, turning her eyes to those who shouted her name, which was a better sight; and then Thelmo spoke, and she leapt down from the shield, as Tekla rode in through a gap in the stockade, bringing what was left of the Wing she led, and halted behind the line.

It needed but a short glance at those of whom Tekla was head, even from one who was little skilled in such war, to see that it was a harder fight than could be long held. Of all those that Elsya had seen when they made flourish before the King, there were but thirty-seven who yet lived, and of these there were few but showed their wounds through the reddened, tooth-torn skins that they wore. Their horses stood with bent heads, breathing hard, as they were drawn up in such array as they might still make, having more wounds than those whose legs were higher than theirs.

170

Thelmo said, "They are spent. They have saved the day, as it is. It is for the footmen now, and for the women, to do what we yet must. I think still that we shall prevail, for they are heartened anew."

Tekla looked at the great plain, on which the swamp-rats swarmed, and at the barrier, jagged and gapped, along which the men and women fought with wearied hands.

"It is not won," she said, "but we must win this fight, you and I." She looked at Thelmo with the understanding which had been theirs from birth. "Will you charge when you see the time?"

His glance answered hers with bewilderment, and then protest, and then assent. To defend as they then did must be death to all at the last, for there was no end to the numbers of those that came, and the sun was still high. They must turn the tide if they could.

He looked again at the remnant of the Left Wing. "You will give them an hour?" he asked. "We can endure for that time."

"No. They will do no more if they learn how weary they are. It is no time for the counting of wounds. I will give them no time at all." Her eyes hardened at the word, and were lit with the exaltation of a great resolve. She turned her horse to ride back to the squadron's head, and as she did this her eyes met those of Elsya, who stood, bravely enough, at Thelmo's side. Elsya thought that they changed to a swift pity, of which she saw not the cause, but, if so, it was gone as soon as it came. Her glance moved to Thelmo's shield, and then to Elsya again. He saw what she meant, though he gave no sign from a doubtful mind.

Tekla rode that charge at the greatest pace that she could yet rouse in a willing horse, with no care for how far behind were those that she led, and they came behind her with levelled spears, at the best they might, for it was their honour that she should not outride them thus, so that she should fall without aid. She rode from side to side through the snapping, squealing horde, doing all the harm that she might, and the rest came at her heels, a bolt of death through the foul, crowding ranks that leapt with tearing jaws or cowered sideways from the trampling feet.

As she came through their midst, Thelmo cast from him a broken sword, and caught up one that was yet sound from a dead hand. He raised it high, calling for all to follow. He leapt over the barrier, striking right and left at the loathly, red-eyed beasts that snapped at him from every side, yet shrank back from the bronze sword that gave death to all that its edge could reach. He called, but none followed at all. Elsya looked at him in a great dread. She came to the edge of the barrier, calling to him to return. At length so he did, there being no use in standing there alone, at a hard fight that he could not longer sustain.

They looked northward, and saw that Tekla was through. They supposed that she would ride inward again by the barrier gap at that point, which should be opened at her need. But she did not do this. She swung the troop round, and must have seen that Thelmo's effort had failed. She charged back through the swamp-rats' ranks.

This time she led the way in a straight course close under the barriers, so that she cleared a space that gave some respite to those who fought on that line. She called something to Thelmo as she passed, pointing to Elsya, who could not hear what it was. She brought her troop clear again, but it was less than before. There were horses that rolled and screamed as they were torn in a score of jaws; there were riders that went to death by the same way, striking still, till their sight failed.

Yet she wheeled again for the third charge, and went in, this time with a throwing of the deadly knives, giving death to those which were too distant for the spears to reach. But this time she did not ride through. She wheeled the troop in the very midst of the foe, turning it as a dog turns that would flatten a smooth bed, and again there was a throwing of knives, that did not cease till there was but one left of the six that had been at the hands of each. There was such slaughter in that crowded place that it gave relief for a minute's length to the barrier fight, drawing the eyes of all that could see. There were rats that turned to run inward to where they thought that the riders of the Left Wing were being ended at last; there were others, of poorer heart, who would be farther from the deadly range of the flying knives and the rush of the sharp-hooved steeds.

Thelmo saw that it would be never, if it were not now. He made level shield. He gave Elsya his other hand, that she should step up. She looked at him with a bloodless face, knowing now what he would do. But she did not draw back her hand. She stepped on to the shield, seating herself with side-drawn feet, as before. He raised her up with a great strength, so that all could see. They went over the barrier, and, with a shout, the whole army of those who fought leapt down in the same way.

Elsya saw that she had led them thus, though they had not followed Thelmo at all. There was a glad pride in her heart, so that she forgot her fear. She rose upright on the shield so that she could be seen afar.

There were some seconds during which she stood thus on the swaying shield. It seemed longer to her. She thought only that it was she who had moved that host, that it was through her that men shouted and smote, and the swamp-rats squealed and gave way. There was a pride in her heart that was more than fear.

Yet fear she must, and with more cause than she had known in her life's length; for the shield swayed and sloped, though Thelmo strove with a giant strength that she should not be overset, taking what wounds he must for that end, and there were those to the right hand and the left who fought well in the same cause. The rats had been in good heart. They had thought that they were near to win. They were hard to turn.

It is not easy to say how their ranks were ruled, yet there must have been those of them who saw that, if Elsya were brought down, the spirit of this charge must fail, and it might be the end of all. For they came together, it may have been a hundred of them, or more, even while their lines broke both to right and left, and while the pressure slackened in that fierce whirlpool of strife where Tekla, with a little group of the Amazons who yet lived, fought on foot against their crowding foes. They came with a rush as of one rat a hundred strong, and Thelmo's bravest, fighting with reddened spears, went down beneath the swarming heap, and stabbed upward the while they died. It was then that the five of the King's guard, who had stood somewhat to the rear, throwing only a knife at times with a sure aim when the need was most, came forward to Thelmo's side. There they fell, giving many deaths as they died, and breaking the force of that rush, as much as they might, being so few.

They gave such aid that Thelmo stood while they lived, though the rats leapt to drag him down from all sides. Yet it was a thing that could not endure. The rats still came on, and those who should have struck for him on either hand were busy with their own deaths on the ground. So the rats leapt and bit. There was one that leapt so that it got its fore-paws on to the shield, its body curving somewhat beneath, and its hind-claws deep in the back of Thelmo's shoulder and neck. Elsya beat at it with her bare hands, and got a clutch of its throat at last, doing bravely enough at this need, but so that the shield shook the more.

Thelmo looked to where his sister yet fought in the little group that was now like a rock that the tide covers higher at every wave, the rats crowding over them from all sides. He thought that her life was done, and his too; but he saw beyond that, that they had bought the great thing for which they had so paid, for the rats gave way on the long front, as far as his sight went. Their lives might be done, yet he would hold Elsya safe as long as he might, though he would not bear her back to the safety of the stockade. She must take her chance at this stake, as a wife should.

So he stood there for a moment more, steadying the shield with his last strength, and heedless of the teeth that drained his life from a dozen wounds. He saw that the tide so turned that he judged that Elsya would be safe if he could endure for a little space, and then he sank to the ground, for a rat bit so that his leg failed.

Elsya went down with a swamp-rat's teeth at her throat. She did not know that she screamed so that her voice reached to Tekla, where she still fought on foot beside a horse that was down with a dozen rat-snouts drinking blood from a torn flank. She knew that her necklace broke in the rat's jaws, and she beat its face with her hands, as it pushed to get a grip under her chin. Thelmo was down at her left side, and she knew that their lives were done, but, with a fierce hatred for that broken toy, she gathered strength to take the beast in her arms, and fling the hinder part of its body over to where Thelmo struggled vainly to gain his feet. As she did this she raised her chin, so that the beast got the grip that it sought, even as she flung its hind-quarters round.

She called out to Thelmo, "Kill this for me!" even as the teeth bit, and she saw his two hands close with a strong grasp on its back, and heard the spine snap. Her eyes laughed over to Thelmo then, so that she did not heed that the blood pulsed from her throat. She saw that his eyes met her own in a good way, and then the beasts hid them, or there was a blur of mist, and it was hard to rule her mind as she would. Knowledge and thought wavered and failed, though she fought to hold them with a stubborn and frightened will, and then a memory came, distant and sharp, a vision of strange and unremembered things, and whether she went from life to death, or from death to life, was a thing that she could not tell.

Tekla, heaving the last rat from Elsya's side on a spear's point, saw surely that she was dead. Thelmo was dead too.

Tekla looked round, and there was none near but those whose fighting had found its end. The rats were in flight at last, and the men and women that had faced death since dawn now followed, and laughed, and slew such as lagged in a wounded way. Tekla looked down at herself, and she knew that her end was near. Life drained from a score of wounds that she had taken as she fought her way to her brother's side. There was none to stanch those streams, and her sight wavered the while she stood.

"I must lie down," she thought, "lest I fall…yet it is a good end for us three."

She lay down at her brother's side. She was glad that they were together in death. Life had been good, though she had missed that which the meanest wins. Her voice came as one who speaks in a dream: "It is the best end that could be."

CHAPTER XLIX.

MISS LEINSTER came into the outer room, where the magician sat at his books. She looked weary and dazed, as one who had come by a hard way.

He looked up, and was glad of that sight. He had not been without fears. Also, when she came back thus, there were good tales to be heard.

"Was it well?"

"It was well enough. I had all I asked, either of caves or trees. I think I have asked for the last time."

He answered, "You may change in that," being wiser than she.

She was slow to speak, so he must do so again. "At least, you have taken no hurt?"

"So you say. I have been Eve in a tree. I have cracked nuts. I have lacked words when a thought came. I have...." She was about to say that she had picked fleas from her own fur, but there were things that were best untold. More than that. Much. She had done things which she could not believe. Yet they were beyond dreams. Was she maid or wife? Her mind went back, and terror came, and a great grief. Can you have grief for a dream?

The magician saw that it would need patience to learn all, which he was eager to do. He said, "It was a very far time."

"It was very near. It is as near as the next room."

He made no answer to that. "Were there men," he asked, "of our own kind?"

"There were men enough, but you had made me an ape." She was sorry when she had said that. It was not a tale to be told. She would say no more.

But she had said too much, or so the magician thought. "Miss Leinster," he said, with reproach, "you have made a wrong charge. I could do no such thing if I would. You could be no less than yourself."

"Well," she said, "it can't be as you will. I did not mean to complain. I will go home."

She rose with a gesture as of one who throws off a cloak which is too heavy to wear. She went out, saying nothing more.

The magician recalled something which he might have thought sooner than he did. "There should have been three." So there were in the end. He had two others to meet in the latter part of that day, at which time there was more said. But we can leave that to itself.

CHAPTER L.

MARGUERITE LEINSTER went to her own home, which was a Mayfair flat on a fifth floor, having no lift, for she was one who would have light and air, even though her legs must work for its gain.

She went first to a desk, where her letters lay. She found one that had been sent on the day on which she had gone by a way of which we know more than most, and she read this, and was well pleased. After that she turned over those that remained, and was discontent. Her hand went to the bell.

"Mildred," she said, when the maid came, "have there been no letters but these? Who has called while I have been away?"

The answer giving her no satisfaction, she must be more explicit. "Mr Cranleigh has not been? That is just as well. I rang to know what you can get me for lunch."

The maid went. Miss Leinster looked no more content than before. She let the other letters lie as they were.

It was evening when Stephen came. She gave him her hand, but was less free with her eyes. She said, when they were seated somewhat apart, "You must have worked hard while I have been away. You look tired."

He met this with, "So do you. You always do when you go away by yourself. I hope this is the last time."

"Perhaps it is. I am glad that you have come to believe at last, and didn't pester Mildred again."

"I don't know what I believe. I'm going to Hungary in a month's time. I've got work that will keep me there, off and on, for the next three years."

"Oh, have you? I'm—glad of that. If it's a good job."

"It's well enough. It will be a good job if you'll come along."

"I might look you up in the spring. I've never seen Hungary yet."

178

"You know I don't mean that. There's plenty of time to get married before we go."

"Not for me."

He rose at that, but made no effort to shorten the distance between them. He leaned moodily against the mantelpiece. "You mean you won't come?"

"I mean I prefer to go where I please, rather than be always bullied by you."

"Then you can damned well stay where you are!"

She recognized the authentic Stephen, who would never leave her alone, and never knew what she wore. She doubted at times if he could have told whether her hair was black or blonde. It was the authentic Stephen, and yet. Well, he had never spoken to her before with quite that brusqueness, even when she had drawn back from a promise which she had almost made.

"So I will," she said, "and I hope you won't come here again, if you're going to talk like that."

"I haven't gone yet. Look here, Marguerite, it's about time that this fooling stopped. You're twenty-eight, if you're a day, and you'd have married me five years ago if I'd the sense to treat you in the right way."

Marguerite rose angrily, though not so much so as she felt that the occasion required. "A thing can't stop that hasn't begun. What fooling do you mean? You won't gain anything by going on like this. Why not sit down and talk sensibly?"

"So I will," he said, "if you'll do the same. You know you'll marry me in the end, and if it isn't time yet, I'd like to know when it will be."

"You know we've had this over a dozen times, and it always ends at the same point. I like to wander about in my own way. I don't want to spend all the year dusting a flat. You haven't even asked me where I've been since you saw me last! "

If this were intended to delay the decision which she recognized as more than usually critical, and which she had not made up her mind how to meet, it was a disastrous error.

"Well," he said, "what's the tale now?"

It was not the words so much as the look he gave which disconcerted her with a memory of things which she must never tell, either to him or to any.

"It's no use," she fenced, "telling you things that you don't believe."

"Oh, I'll believe right enough."

"There isn't much to tell," she said weakly. "It was a very primitive time. I don't think it could have been real."

"Anyone to knock you on the head with a club?"

"No, of course not. It was just caves and trees, and…and things like that."

"Ever come down from the trees?"

"Yes, of course."

"Without being fetched?"

"Yes, of course."

"So I thought. You must have got worse since then."

There was a moment's silence after that, and then Stephen added, "You're not telling me very much. Not very lucid, is it?"

"I've told you other times and you wouldn't believe, so what's the good?"

"But I will this time."

"How can you tell till you've heard?"

Stephen didn't answer to that. He was looking at the bare forearm that was offered to his inspection by a short-sleeved dress. He seemed to have noticed something at last!

"Anything wrong with my arm?"

"The colour hasn't changed."

Miss Leinster looked puzzled, as she was. Did he mean her dress? But his eyes had been on her arm. She was sure of that. Her arm had some downy hairs, very fine, but somewhat longer than are usual, and which would have been more conspicuous had they been of a darker colour. She knew that it was somewhat hairier than a girl's arm usually is, and was never sure that this singularity pleased her. She had been accustomed to settle the doubt with a razor, but she had been careless of late, or there seemed to have been some growth during the last fortnight. Suddenly she knew what he meant. The colour was the same. But how could he know, or guess? It was incredible, and yet she felt that he knew. But how much? She would have given anything she possessed to stop the blush which seemed to get worse as she raged inwardly that she could not control it. What could he know? It was absurd.

"I think you're hateful," she said.

"I think you're just the opposite." He did not seem perturbed by her outburst. He seemed to be enjoying himself much better than he had done a few minutes earlier. He added, in a tone and words in which he might have been better practised to his own advantage, "I think you're just lovely."

She was not mollified by this compliment. Incident after incident came to her mind. Did he know that…and that? How could he? It was absurd. "I wish you'd go," she said furiously.

"If you'd kindly tell me what I've done wrong. I don't want to carry you all the way to Hungary. Elsie says you were such a weight that she thought I was going to throw you down more than once during the afternoon."

"Elsya. Elsie says? What can she…? Stephen, it was no more than a dream. Unless it's still going on. Tell me just what do you know, and how." She spoke now with a nervous earnestness, such as he had never known her to show. She looked at him with frightened eyes.

"I know everything. You didn't think that three could play at that game."

"But it was no more than a dream."

"Well, we dreamed the same."

"And Elsie? Elsie knows everything?"

"No, I shouldn't say that. She doesn't know…." He mentioned things which were known to themselves only, which were too intimate to be told when they occurred, or to be detailed now. "And if you think," he ended, "I'm going to Hungary alone after all that, well, you're just wrong. So the question is, Will you come quiet, as the police say, or have you got to be carried again?"

She broke into a sudden smile, which brought back to its own place the dimple which we had occasion to notice when we saw her first. She met his eyes at last with an invitation in her own which he had never seen there before.

"Yes," she said, "I suppose I shall." But which she meant is not as clear as we should have liked it to be.

ABOUT THE AUTHOR

SYDNEY FOWLER WRIGHT (1874-1965) penned over seventy volumes of science fiction, fantasy, classic mysteries, historical novels, poetry, and non-fiction, many of them being published by the Borgo Press Imprint of Wildside Press.